"I don't date clients, Mr. Adler."

"Hotel policy," Jennie added untruthfully. The policy was her own, but she still thought it was a good one.

"Does that mean I have to take my business to the Ritz?" Wes joked, astonished by her blunt answer.

"That's up to you, but I don't date strangers, either."

"We're not strangers. We're acquaintances. Up until a minute ago we were on a first-name basis." Wes cocked his head to one side as he watched her retreat. "Jennie!" he called.

He saw her stop at the door and look over her shoulder. He read the impatience in her flashing green eyes and said, "If dinner is out, how about lunch someday?"

She shook her head. "Don't be difficult, Mr. Adler."

"Anything to oblige. Will it be okay if I'm impossible?"

Dear Reader,

Welcome to Silhouette—experience the magic of the wonderful world where two people fall in love. Meet heroines that will make you cheer for their happiness, and heroes (be they the boy next door or a handsome, mysterious stranger) who will win your heart. Silhouette Romance reflects the magic of love—sweeping you away with books that will make you laugh and cry, heartwarming, poignant stories that will move you time and time again.

In the coming months we're publishing romances by many of your all-time favorites, such as Diana Palmer, Brittany Young, Sondra Stanford and Annette Broadrick. Your response to these authors and our other Silhouette Romance authors has served as a touchstone for us, and we're pleased to bring you more books with Silhouette's distinctive medley of charm, wit and—above all—*romance*.

I hope you enjoy this book and the many stories to come. Experience the magic!

Sincerely,

Tara Hughes
Senior Editor
Silhouette Books

JOAN SMITH

It Takes Two

Silhouette *Romance*

Published by Silhouette Books New York

America's Publisher of Contemporary Romance

SILHOUETTE BOOKS
300 E. 42nd St., New York, N.Y. 10017

ISBN: 0-373-08656-3

First Silhouette Books printing June 1989

Printed in the U.S.A.

Books by Joan Smith

Silhouette Romance

JOAN SMITH

has written many Regency romances but likes working with the greater freedom of contemporaries. She also enjoys mysteries and Gothics, collects Japanese porcelain and is a passionate gardener. A native of Canada, she is the mother of three.

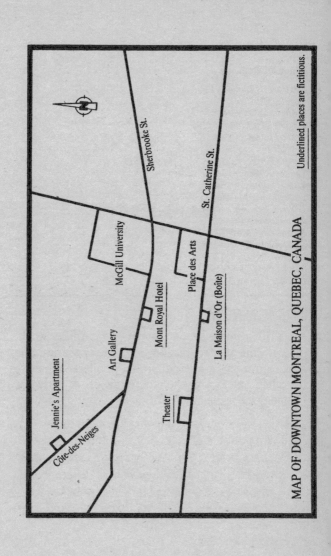

MAP OF DOWNTOWN MONTREAL, QUEBEC, CANADA

Underlined places are fictitious.

Sherbrooke St.

St. Catherine St.

McGill University

Place des Arts

Mont Royal Hotel

Art Gallery

La Maison d'Or (Boîte)

Jennie's Apartment

Côte-des-Neiges

Theater

Chapter One

Improvise, Ms. Longman. Improvise, *c'est tout*!" Mr. Simon said, with a shrug. Mr. Simon, although he had very little French vocabulary, liked to sprinkle a few foreign phrases in deference to his adopted city, Montreal.

"I'll see what I can do," Jennie Longman replied.

"Don't see, just do it. If Olympia Films wants an entire floor of the Mont Royal Hotel for a week, they shall have an entire floor for a week. They're here for the opening of their new movie. The arrival of Blanche Laure will be televised. You can't buy that kind of publicity," he informed Jennie. "The Ritz Carlton will be furious!"

"Olympia's sending their liaison, a Mr. Benson, at two this afternoon to finalize arrangements," Simon continued. "I wish I could attend to him personally, but I have a meeting of the board of directors. You can handle Benson?"

"Certainly, Mr. Simon."

"With kid gloves, *il va sans dire*," he cautioned, and strode majestically from her office. Jennie winced at his pronunciation, but he was at least making an attempt to speak French.

Jennie's boss always reminded her of a rooster, with his beaky nose and cocky strut—although he preened and primped more like a peacock. Mr. Simon took a keen interest in his appearance. His sandy hair was arranged to blow-dried perfection. His navy blue custom-tailored suit was accessorized with a discreet tie of French design and he always wore Italian shoes.

Improvising would be no easy task, but a concierge never used the word "impossible." Jennie would just have to rearrange the upcoming bookings and attempt to make Olympia Films happy. She retrieved the reservations book from the front desk and began to studiously examine it.

World-class director Wescott Adler was the major shareholder of Olympia Films, therefore Jennie decided to give him the largest bedroom with sitting room en suite. His various assistants and PR personnel would occupy the single rooms. She saved the most difficult room assignment for last. Blanche Laure was the star of the movie and she would obviously require something special in the way of accommodations. Jennie decided it would be best to discuss those details with Mr. Benson during their meeting.

Meanwhile, Jennie studied the newspapers to see what she could learn about Olympia's latest project. It was part of a concierge's job to know her clients, to try and anticipate their needs. Though his name appeared prominently in news articles, there were no pictures of Wescott Adler. The lovely face of Blanche Laure garnered the attention of the press. She had a classically perfect face and a beautiful mane of black hair growing in a widow's peak

from her white forehead. But her eyes were what gave
Blanche her star quality. Large and luminous, they spoke
of fragility and vulnerability.

Jennie had suffered through many a melodramatic hour
in dark theaters with the infamous actress. Jennie wondered what she would be like in real life, then turned her
attention to the article. *Orphan of the Storm*, the new film
release starring Ms. Laure, was being premiered in Montreal. The movie had been shot in northern Quebec. The
wild terrain served as a perfect location for the recreation
of a ravaged Europe after the Napoleonic wars. But why
not premiere such a big film in L.A.?

Jennie read on. The premiere was a big boost not only
for the hotel but for Montreal's reputation, as well. Thus
far, Toronto had been getting most of the American
movies that were being made in Canada, despite the fact
that Montreal—the second largest French-speaking city in
the world—was more cosmopolitan. It was a beautiful
place, combining old-world charm with the fast-paced
excitement of the new world.

Jennie's reading was interrupted by Mr. Bradley in
Room 711, who had requested a large-sized muumuu and
a lei of silk flowers. "I'll do my best, Mr. Bradley." It was
a tall order to fill in Montreal, in the middle of January.

Three-quarters of Jennie's noon hour was spent finding these unlikely objects. A concierge didn't ask prying
questions, but she had her suspicions about the Bradleys.
Her suspicion was that Mr. Bradley, a buyer for a bath-
ing suit company, had taken a holiday with his mistress by
pretending to have gone to Hawaii on business and now
wanted a present to take home to his wife. Jennie ruefully admitted that being a concierge often revealed to her
the seamy side of human nature.

Of course, the job had its perks, too. The work was varied and interesting, the pay was excellent, the tips were even better and she met such exciting people. What other job would give her an opportunity to meet a movie legend like Blanche Laure? She took the silk lei and muumuu up to Mr. Bradley, for which she received a generous tip.

It was one forty-five, and Mr. Benson from Olympia Films was scheduled for a two o'clock appointment. Jennie tidied her office and examined it with a proud, proprietary air. Her office had an old, carved mahogany desk, brass fixtures and a Persian carpet. Unlike the newer flashy hotel chains, the Mont Royal was an elegant but very discreet establishment, possessing the old-world charm characteristic of some European hotels.

Not bad for twenty-four years. She had grown up on a farm, where she had learned French from her Mom and English from her Dad, and being bilingual helped. Her varied employment background as everything from a sales clerk to travel agent to stenographer had struck Mr. Simon to be more than satisfactory. And now here she was, sitting behind a massive desk in an elegant office in one of the ritziest hotels in Montreal—about to arrange a visit for famous show-biz people.

Before Mr. Benson arrived, she decided to slip into her private washroom to repair her makeup. For a more mature and professional appearance, Jennie wore her thick chestnut hair pulled back in a French braid. It lent a touch of distinction to her rather gamine face. She had green eyes which were a trifle slanted at the outer edge; her small nose and a slightly pointed chin were almost feline and rather exotic. But the severe hair style and the conservative hotel uniform made her look perfectly businesslike and efficient.

The severity of her uniform, a navy suit, was softened by a white silk blouse with a bow tie in front. Jennie always wore a fresh rosebud on her lapel, beside the gold crossed-keys pin that was a badge of her profession. She was a registered member of Les Clefs d'Or, the prestigious international association of concierges. Only a hundred and twenty people were actually registered members. It practically guaranteed a job in any large city in North America, or the western world, providing she could learn the language of the country.

Jennie didn't intend to stay at the Mont Royal forever. She wanted to travel around the continent and maybe eventually move to Europe. She straightened the brass plaque on her desk. It was inscribed J.M. Longman. She lifted it, polishing away a few motes of dust. While she was straightening a few things in the office, her buzzer sounded and the secretary said, "Mr. Benson is here, Ms. Longman. May I show him in?"

"Certainly," Jennie said, and hurried to her chair so she could rise up and make the client feel important when he entered. She hardly knew what to expect. A liaison, working for a movie company, he'd probably be a nervous ball of energy, speaking in the industry lingo unknown to her, and he would probably start out demanding the moon and stars. He'd be wearing a golden tan, sunglasses and some outlandishly stylish clothes.

The door opened and the secretary ushered a man in who exceeded her wildest expectations. From the large slouch hat pulled low over his eyes to the mink-lined coat hanging loose at his shoulders, he was a perfect model of overstatement. He was colossal, stupendous, boffo, and he would probably utter all of those silly words within minutes.

Jennie rose and offered her hand, saying, "I'm Ms. Longman, the hotel concierge. And you're Mr. Benson?" She managed to control the smile.

"Just call me R.K.," he replied, and removed the hat. He tossed it with careless accuracy onto one of the pegs of her brass coat tree. With the hat gone, Jennie saw he was not only tanned but oiled against the harsh winter winds, which gave his face a sheen. It was hard to imagine what he looked like under those wraparound sunglasses, but his hair was a honey blond and frizzy.

"I usually deal with the CEO," he informed her, in a bored voice.

"I beg your pardon?"

"Chief Executive Officer. You *do* have a manager here?"

Jennie bit her tongue to withhold a snappish reply. "The manager's busy at the moment, but I'll do everything I can to help you. May I take your coat, R.K.?" she asked.

He turned for her to remove it. She was tempted to toss it at the coat rack, but propriety was second nature, and she carried it, admiring the mink lining. It must be nice and warm, she thought.

"What a lovely coat." She smiled.

"I picked that little number up here in Canada," he told her. "I don't know how you people stand the weather. You must have thick hides." On this speech he sat down and threw one leg over the other. "Seems like a nice little hotel," he said, glancing around with mild approval.

"Thank you. The premier of France was satisfied when he stayed here last month. We're small but quite exclusive. We'll try to satisfy all your requirements."

"That's what we're paying you for, dear." The words were patronizing, but the expression was friendly. "You know, you remind me of someone," R.K. said pensively. "A young Judy Garland, is it? No, the nose isn't right. Who could it be?"

"How interesting. Now, about your requirements," Jennie said briskly.

"You realize we'll all have to be on one floor. The logistics are my department. We'll be doing a lot of meetings, and I don't want the group spread all over the place. These boots were made for walking, not running." He examined his tooled leather boots with interest. "Of course I'm used to inconvenience, coming from L.A. The place is a maze. L.A. *is* a great big freeway."

Jennie's reply was designed to draw him back to work, and also to let him know that while the Mont Royal didn't have a whole floor unreserved, it was willing to oblige him. "The rooms have already been taken care of." She smiled.

"That's what I like to hear. Item two, price. No problem. We go first class all the way."

"Good, our prices are reasonable. I'll give you the rates with some other literature I've prepared. There is just one thing..." The dark glasses turned to face her. The sunlight struck them, turning R.K. Benson into a parody of a creature from outer space, with glowing orbs and a frizzed halo. "It's about Ms. Laure," Jennie said.

"Has she been in touch with you already?" he asked nervously.

"No, the problem—though not a serious one—is where to put her. You indicated you wanted all the rooms on one floor. Mr. Adler wants a sitting room as well as a bedroom."

"Absolutely. Adler is top priority, *numero uno*."

"The fifth floor, the only one I could vacate, has only one double room. I was just wondering where we might put Miss Laure." She frowned at the floor plan as she spoke.

"Let's see what we've got," Mr. Benson said, and rose languidly to peer over her shoulder. As he traced the floor plan with one carefully manicured finger, Jennie noticed the heavy scent of musk.

"I've tentatively penciled Ms. Laure into the second largest room, two doors away from Mr. Adler," she explained.

"N.G. No good. *Nyet*. That will definitely have to be changed. They'll want to be next to each other. And Blanche will want me on her other side. Strictly platonic in the latter case," he added, with a cynical laugh.

Jennie took the idea that the relationship was not strictly platonic between Ms. Laure and Adler. They would want the appearance of separate rooms, perhaps, while sleeping together. She knew Ms. Laure had gone through several husbands in her long career. Her present marital status was unclear. Jennie pointed to the rooms on either side of Mr. Adler's and said, "Unfortunately, these rooms would hardly do for Ms. Laure."

She heard an amused snort, and peered up. "We're talking mega-star here, J.M." Jennie had to think a minute to realize she was J.M. He had obviously read her brass nameplate. "Laure is boffo at the box office. Her clothes wouldn't fit in that cubbyhole. Clothes? Did I say *clothes*? It wouldn't hold her shoes."

Jennie quickly made her decision. "The other alternative is to break up the group. We're pretty heavily booked, but we have a deluxe penthouse suite. It serves royalty and honeymooners and any VIP who happens to be staying with us. I was going to suggest it, but perhaps Ms. Laure and Mr. Adler will want to be—closer together,'' she said discreetly.

Mr. Benson considered it a moment. "If Laure ever found out that suite was vacant or, saints forbid, if some other actress should move in while she's here she'd have my head on a platter. Put her in the penthouse, and I'll square it with Adler later. You can impress on Laure that she has the finest suite in the hotel,'' he added.

Jennie was beginning to get the idea that Ms. Laure was going to require the best of everything. "I'm sure she'll be happy with it. It's furnished in genuine Louis XIV, with priceless Aubusson carpets.''

"That sounds like Blanche's style,'' he nodded, unimpressed. "And she's bringing Ruby for company, so perhaps she can do without Adler on top of her. No double entendre intended,'' he added, with a bored smile.

Jennie gave him a glacial look and glanced at her list. "We don't have a Ruby listed.''

"Her chihuahua,'' Mr. Benson explained, with an air of amusement. "Ruby—a pearl beyond price, but if you want the numbers, try two thou. That's what she paid for the dog.''

"But we don't allow pets in the rooms,'' Jennie said. This was perilously close to saying "impossible.'' There was stiff competition among the elite hotels in Montreal, just hoping for the chance to extend their hospitality to celebrities like Blanche Laure. Mr. Simon had warned her to use kid gloves. "Well, I suppose for Ms. Laure we could make an exception,'' she said reluctantly. It was the priceless carpets that worried her.

Mr. Benson's thin lips lifted almost imperceptibly. "Naturally,'' he said. "Bear in mind, at all times, that for Ms. Laure, we must all make exceptions. Incidentally, I should mention that she's a vegetarian.''

Jennie jotted it down on her pad. "No problem there. Our chef is experienced at preparing all types of cuisine. Are there any other idiosyncrasies I should know about?"

"Do you have an hour or two?" Mr. Benson asked, but didn't wait for an answer. "She'll have her own coiffeur with her, but she'll want the best masseur in town. That's masseur, not masseuse, you get my meaning?"

"Yes, I understand."

"Jot down a list of the better jewelers and fashion boutiques. We'll want to know what shows are currently playing. I'm referring to live theater, obviously."

"*Mother Courage* is running. It's a sellout, so if you want tickets..."

"Oh, no, not Bertie Brecht. He's passé. Blanche likes musicals." He looked at Jennie hopefully.

"Nothing at the moment, sorry."

"I must remember I'm not in L.A. now. Blanche will have to rough it with the rest of us." Jennie tried to conceal her bristling mood. "Have the best doctor and dentist in town on call, and keep your fingers crossed that we won't have to use them."

Jennie had the idea that Mr. Benson was trying to impress her, but she remained unfazed. "All that is standard procedure, R.K.," she said blandly. "Have you any unusual requests?"

"We'll want plenty of mesquite for the steaks. Ordinary wood won't do, don't even think of letting your chef use charcoal. Have plenty of Perrier water in supply, and we'll want to try some of Montreal's famous French cuisine while we're here," he said, tapping his polished nails on the desk.

Jennie jotted. "No problem. Will you be wanting a boardroom for meetings?"

"Adler wants a boardroom scheduled for our exclusive use."

"What size of group will you want to accommodate?"

"Not more than a dozen, but you'd better make it large enough to set up a projector. Adler will bring his own equipment if he plans to view anything.

"Adler will have his own secretary, and I'll be looking after Laure's needs personally. I'm liaising for her on this film."

"I'll just give you some of our brochures. We can make travel arrangements for you or arrange sightseeing tours, get show tickets, flowers, whatever. Oh, I expect you'll be wanting champagne and flowers in Ms. Laure's suite?"

"Rightie-ho. Glad you reminded me. Dom Pérignon '57, four dozen red roses—have them addressed to 'The Divine Blanche.' Sign that, Wescott. No, make it 'Love, Wes.' Oh, and a very small filet mignon, medium rare, with mushrooms, ten minutes after arrival.'

Jennie wrote furiously to keep up with him. "I thought Ms. Laure was a vegetarian?" she asked in surprise.

"They're for Ruby."

"A filet mignon for a *dog*?"

Benson smiled at having surprised her. It put him in a good mood, and he became quite communicative. "Medium rare, with mushrooms. I'll make sure you receive Ruby's sterling silver dog bowl before dinnertime. She won't eat from anything else. Blanche really should get busy and have a child while there's still time. It's ludicrous to lavish so much affection on a dumb animal. By dumb I don't mean to infer the animal is either stupid or mute. *Au contraire*! She barks up a storm. Blanche tells me Ruby has a canine I.Q. of a hundred and fifty, which makes her about three times as bright as her owner. You didn't hear that from me, J.M.,'' he smiled. "Oh, is there a good dog psychiatrist in the city?''

"Yes, as a matter of fact we had a cat with a persecution complex last year. I'll leave Doctor Latimer's number with Ms. Laure.''

"Only if she asks for it. Let's not encourage her,'' he said, adopting a conspiratorial tone.

"Is there anything else?''

"Yes, keep a hospitality suite open for us, and we'd like to hire your largest party room for the evening of the opening. Cocktails before the show and a big buffet after. Lobster, oysters, caviar—the works. We'll settle on the menu when I return. Remind me,'' he added. "Mr. Adler will want to speak to you shortly after our arrival, as well. Perhaps some arrangements for the press . . .''

"I take it you have no objection to the press knowing you'll be here?'' she asked.

"The more press, the better Blanche. Free publicity is so much sweeter than the kind you have to pay for. Rightie-ho.'' Mr. Benson rose and Jennie got his coat. He turned for her to drop it on his shoulders. "We'll be arriving Monday at two. That gives you nearly a week of ghastly preparations, poor girl. *Arrivederci*.'' He stopped and quirked his head to one side. "Wrong language. I'm in Quebec today. It's *au revoir*, isn't it, *chérie*?''

He chucked her under the chin. Jennie twitched her head away. "My, my, aren't we touchy?'' he said.

He adjusted his glasses, put on his slouch hat and swept out of her office. Jennie closed the door and sat at her desk, thoroughly distraught. Between the dog with an I.Q. of 150, who ate from sterling silver, a vegetarian prima donna who was having an affair with her director and a whole slew of men as impossible as R.K. Benson, it promised to be a difficult visit. In fact, if the liaison was this big a jerk, what would the great Wescott Adler be like? It didn't bear thinking about.

When Mr. Simon returned from the board meeting, he stopped at Jennie's office for a briefing. He seemed more interested in what Mr. Benson wore and how he behaved than in the list of preparations. She knew he was a movie fan. "A mink-lined coat!" he exclaimed, and asked for other details.

She finally got down to business. "I'm a little worried about having a dog in the penthouse with those Aubusson carpets. I think I'll replace them," she said.

"We'll leave them. What harm can a little chihuahua do?"

"If you say so," she said doubtfully. Mr. Simon was the boss. "The only other item that bothers me is getting tickets for shows that are sold out. Mr. Benson didn't seem to think Ms. Laure would want to see *Mother Courage*, but the new version is the hottest ticket in town. I would imagine an actress of Blanche's caliber would want to see it. I really should start twisting arms now."

"You wouldn't know what night to get, though."

"That's why I haven't done anything. I wouldn't mind seeing it myself if they couldn't use the tickets, but not at a hundred bucks a seat, and that's what the scalpers are asking for them."

"Better leave it. You may have to work some overtime, Ms. Longman. I trust you have nothing desperately urgent planned next week?"

"I'll clear my calendar, Mr. Simon. I think the show here at the Mont Royal is going to be as amusing as any in town."

"Good. And you can call me P.S., Ms. Longman." He gave an embarrassed smile. "When in Rome, you know."

"Rightie-ho, P.S.," she smiled.

Mr. Simon, that model of formality, smiled. "I sound like a postscript. I'd use my other initial, but that would make me P.U. My middle name is Ulrich."

It was the first time Jennie remembered hearing him make a joke. Something about this particular visit was beginning to change people already. Mr. Simon hadn't even been this jubilant when they had members of the royal family visiting last summer. The excitement proved to be contagious.

She was surprised at the time—it was five-thirty already. The afternoon had sped by.

Chapter Two

Over the next week, Jennie had her usual duties to occupy her, many of which involved making arrangements for Olympia Films. Some members of a European royal family were expected in a few months, the committees for the reelection of the mayor had given a fund-raising dinner and Arthur Makepiece, a best-selling writer, was coming to give a lecture series. The chef was told to obtain a supply of mesquite, the arrangement for the boardroom was accomplished with no problem and the various services Blanche Laure might require were lined up.

The nerves of all the hotel employees began tightening early on the day of the Olympia group's arrival. They were expected at two in the afternoon. Jennie inspected the penthouse suite personally at one-thirty, finding the roses and Dom Pérignon in place. The only item missing was Ruby's silver bowl. It hadn't arrived, and Jennie had a substitute bowl standing by. Not sterling, but silver-plated. Surely a dog wouldn't know the difference.

When she came downstairs, some members of the media had arrived and were coordinating locations for press sessions with Mr. Simon. The pace of the hotel quickened noticeably. The porters were on the alert, and the dining room staff was ready to serve food at short notice. Other guests of the hotel had heard rumors and were beginning to huddle around the lobby, whispering. Photographers paced back and forth at the main entrance hoping for a shot of Blanche Laure. There was an air of expectancy so strong Jennie could feel it.

Two o'clock came and went. Of course it was unrealistic to think they'd arrive from Los Angeles at the stroke of two. It was two-fifteen, two-thirty, and still no arrivals. The photographers began grumbling. Jennie took a fresh ice bucket upstairs for the Dom Pérignon. She wanted everything to be perfect.

At three o'clock, the doorman peeked his head in the door and announced, "They're coming. A whole cavalcade of limousines!" Then he rushed back to his post to open car doors.

Mr. Simon was resplendent in a new suit and fresh haircut. The aura of his expensive and powerful scent was overwhelming. It seemed to grow headier every time he appeared. Jennie thought he must have been giving himself another spray every time he went into his office. He tugged nervously at his shirt cuffs and tie, and ran a hand over his hair.

"*I'll* welcome Blanche Laure, Ms. Longman," he said. "You remain in the lobby, but you stand right here. Just be ready to help if I need you. Oh, she's here!" His pale face turned pink and his eyes glowed with pleasure.

Jennie kept her place in the background and stared, like everyone else, at the legendary Blanche Laure. She swooped in, carrying in her arms a noisy little chihuahua, wearing a rather chic red turtleneck sweater. Jennie was surprised the star wasn't wearing fur, but the black velvet hooded cape with scarlet satin lining was very dramatic.

At close range, it was obvious that Blanche was no longer young, but she was still lovely. Her hair was still a glossy black, probably with the help of dye, growing in that pronounced peak from her forehead. Her soulful eyes were heavily layered with false eyelashes and adorned with a great deal of makeup. The lobby was hushed, as if everyone present was waiting for a miracle.

When Blanche entered a room all eyes were on her, but it occurred to Jennie that Mr. Adler was paying the bill and should be greeted, too. Mr. Simon was so excited to meet Blanche Laure that he couldn't be counted on to do it. She scanned the throng, but no one seemed to stand out from the others, except perhaps R.K. Benson in his slouch hat and mink-lined coat.

At the doorway, Blanche stopped and looked around while flash bulbs popped and TV cameras whirred. With one graceful hand she lifted back her hood and posed for more pictures. She made a show of just touching the chihuahua's lips to her cheek. When she had endured enough pictures, Blanche raised her hand. It seemed to Jennie that no one breathed, in fear of missing Blanche's first words. Mr. Simon took it as his cue to dart forward and welcome her.

"Miss Laure—allow me to present myself. I'm Mr. Simon, the manager, at your service. Do call me P.S. On behalf of the Mont Royal, I welcome you to Montreal." He bowed obsequiously, offering his right hand. As

Blanche held Ruby in her left arm, she allowed him to shake her right one, but she didn't smile. She just looked, with those great, dark eyes.

Ruby barked. Miss Laure sniffed the air. "What is that awful stench?" she demanded. "It's making Ruby ill. Take us to our rooms at once, and deliver Ruby's steak, medium rare."

Jennie had finally heard the great Blanche speak. Her voice was husky, a throbbing one that sent chills down the spine, but her words were a letdown. Jennie could hardly believe that the legendary actress lacked the grace and charm she exuded on the screen. The word rude didn't seem too strong.

There was a flash of scarlet as the tail of her cape swooshed aside, knocking over a vase of roses on a side table. Ms. Laure ignored it. She looked over her shoulder and said, "Wes, darling. My room, right away. We won't want to be disturbed. The elevator?" She cast an imperious look at Mr. Simon.

"Right this way, Miss Laure." He bowed again, and accompanied her. "It's a great honor to have you with us, Miss Laure. I've enjoyed all your films." Blanche didn't answer.

Jennie unglued her eyes from Miss Laure and looked to see which man Blanche had called Wes. That would be Wescott Adler, the director. She counted three women, R.K. Benson, and half a dozen tanned clones, donning sun-glasses, but none of them went scurrying after Blanche. The man who detached himself from the pack had been following her at a leisurely pace looking like a sailor on leave. He was the most subdued person in the group. Jennie had mistaken him for a bodyguard. But once Blanche made her exit, the pressmen ran after him.

He was a tall, wide-shouldered man who walked with the rolling gait of a sailor. Or perhaps it was his black turtleneck and navy pea jacket that brought that comparison to mind. His hair was jet black, and he wore it slightly long. He turned to the waiting pressmen and said, "Don't come upstairs till I call you. Have a drink while you're waiting—my treat." His voice was low-pitched and unhurried. Almost lazy.

Jennie stood, startled to realize this was the famous director, Wescott Adler. His face was weathered, but more ruddy than tanned. A second look showed her an air of authority in the upward tilt of his firm chin and strong jaw. He didn't wear sunglasses. His eyes were a soft, dove gray color, that stood out dramatically on his face. No one called him W.A.

He cast a curious look around the lobby, stopping when he spotted Jennie's uniform. He took a step toward her and said, "No calls for Ms. Laure for the next few hours."

Jennie said, "Yes sir," and forgot to welcome him formally.

Wes went into the elevator, the door closed, then Mr. Simon came forward, smiling and rubbing his hands. "Well, this is going to be an exciting week. Give the order to the chef for the steak, Ms. Longman, and you'd better call housekeeping to clean up that spilled vase. A stupid place to leave flowers. See that it's removed at once."

The small table with its welcoming Sèvres vase of roses was a fixture at the Mont Royal. It had stood in the same spot for years, but of course Miss Laure was not to be accused of carelessness in knocking it over. Jennie went into her office to make the necessary calls. She reminded the kitchen to send up Ruby's steak. It was promptly sent down again, accompanied by the silver bowl. Couldn't the woman put the steak in the bowl herself?

Jennie was beginning to see what R.K. meant by saying they must all make allowances for Blanche. Another idol bit the dust. But as concierge, she was used to dealing with self-important clients, and tried to shrug this experience off. She went on with her other duties, but noticed that reporters and photographers had waited close to an hour before they were called up to Blanche's suite, although they were only allotted fifteen minutes for interviews. Thoughtless, inconsiderate...what had Blanche and Wescott Adler been doing up there for an hour? As if she didn't know! In the midst of her silent tirade, Jennie's phone rang.

"The concierge's office. Ms. Longman speaking," she said.

"Wes Adler here." Jennie stifled a little gasp of surprise, and braced herself for whatever unreasonable request he might make. "Can I see you for a minute?" he asked.

"Certainly, Mr. Adler. Shall I go to Ms. Laure's room?"

"No, my room."

"I'll be right up."

She hung up and sat thinking for a moment before leaving. Now what could he want? Did he have to drag her upstairs to order a drink or something to eat? Most celebrities were a royal pain in the neck, and movie stars promised to be the worst of the lot. Determined to be pleasant and helpful at all times, Jennie wore a smile when she tapped on his door.

"Come!" he called. She stepped in, to find Mr. Adler just coming out of the bathroom. He wore the fleecy white terry cloth robe the hotel supplied and was toweling his hair dry. It stuck up in spikes all over, removing that air of arrogance she had noticed before.

"Hi!" He smiled, and walked forward to shake her hand. His was warm and large. As he engulfed hers in a firm grasp he said, "Wescott Adler, you're—" He recognized her from the lobby. In her uniform and braided hair she seemed to him a caricature of a female soldier. Why did this green-eyed girl with the kittenish face behave so stiffly? As a director, he mentally cast interesting people he met in roles he felt best suited them. He would have cast this bright-eyed young lady as a fairy princess.

A rather strict fairy princess. She had pokered up when Blanche knocked the vase over. Maybe it was an expensive one. He sensed the air of withdrawal in her. She seemed annoyed that he was holding her hand so long. She would probably be more helpful if he charmed her into line.

"Ms. Longman, the concierge," Jennie said stiffly. His fingers tightened on hers, just before he released them.

"I just wanted to congratulate you on a job well done and thank you. Everything's just as we asked, except for Ruby's bowl." His smile was more than polite. It was friendly, without being suggestive.

"Mr. Benson said he'd give it to us, but he didn't send it ahead," Jennie pointed out swiftly.

"Relax, Ms. Longman. That wasn't an accusation, just a comment. Ms. Laure couldn't send it prior to our arrival or Ruby would have starved. She won't eat out of anything else." He tossed the towel aside and went to the mirror to comb his hair. Still wet from the shower, it lay in a glistening cap on his head. "I'd like you to recommend the best night spot," he said over his shoulder.

"We have an excellent dining room," she replied.

"Let me rephrase that," he said, and setting the comb aside, he turned to face her. He wore a laughing expression. "We want the biggest, brightest, most popular spot in town. Where will Blanche be seen by the most people?"

"Les Copains on St. Catherine Street has a popular floor show."

"Good, make reservations for a party of twelve—tell them it's for Blanche Laure."

"Certainly, Mr. Adler." She needed no instructions in how to perform her job! For that matter, the concierge of one of the finest hotels in town carried some prestige, too.

He studied her a moment with his penetrating, gray eyes. "My friends call me Wes," he said. "What do your friends call you, Ms. Longman?"

"Jennie. Or J.M., if you prefer."

He ignored the initials. "Jennie," he repeated, gazing at her to set the name in his mind. It suited her, a down-to-earth, no-nonsense name. "About the vase Blanche broke while making her grand entrance, just put it and any other destruction my crew may wreak on the bill." He gestured toward his sitting room and Jennie followed him in.

"Is there anything else, Mr.—Wes?" she asked, glancing at her watch to let him know she had other things to do.

He observed her little trick, but offered her a seat. She sat down, primly straightening her skirt over her delightful-looking knees. His eyes flickered lower to her neat, shapely ankles. "Yes, I'd like tickets for *Mother Courage* tomorrow night." That should rattle her, he thought, knowing it would be difficult.

He saw the look of despair that settled on her face, and laughed. "I also want the moon on a platter, if it's not too much trouble. Is that out of the question?"

"Nothing's impossible," she said weakly, "if the price is right."

"Montreal sounds a lot like Hollywood," he murmured, with a look askance from the corner of his eyes. She didn't care for the innuendo in his tone. "It might help if you use my name," he suggested. She didn't much care for that, either.

"I have my own sources," she replied, a little curtly. "It's been sold out for weeks, but I'll see what I can do. How many tickets..." She looked fearful of his answer.

"Two. I realize that it would be unreasonable to expect a block of tickets. What other sights do you recommend seeing in the city, Jennie?"

Jennie mentioned the various celebrities who were appearing at the local clubs. There were some big names, but none of them seemed to impress Mr. Adler.

"I was thinking of more unique settings. I can see all the entertainers in L.A. or Vegas. What are the famous landmarks? To give you an idea what I mean, if it were San Francisco I'd want to see Fisherman's Wharf, Lombard Street, Nob Hill."

"Oh, you want a tour of the city!" Jennie was surprised, pleasantly so, to discover there was one rational member in the movie group. "I can arrange that with no trouble."

"I'm not much for organized tours," he said. "I don't necessarily want to see every old church in the city in one afternoon. I like to browse in my spare moments, poke around a new place and learn its secrets. If your—" he hesitated a moment. "If your boyfriend were visiting for a few days, where would you take him?" As an afterthought, he added, "Or does he live in Montreal?"

Jennie noticed the hesitation over the last question. "No, he doesn't." It was none of his business if she didn't have a boyfriend.

"I noticed a big green dome as we drove into town," he mentioned. "What's that?"

"St. Joseph's Oratory. It's a famous shrine, dedicated to Brother André." She looked to see if he would balk at a religious monument.

He nodded, interested, and said, "What would you show—your boyfriend?"

"I'd probably show him McGill University, the Beaux Arts, the Museum of Fine Art. I'd take him on the subway—ours is clean, safe and quiet," she said proudly.

"That'll be a change," he nodded. Jennie wasn't sure whether he was making fun of her, so she chose to ignore it.

"I'd take him to the top of Mount Royal to watch the skating and skiing. Oh, and Westmount, the Nob Hill of Montreal, with *beautiful* old mansions. Then I'd take him to the east end of the city, to see the French part of town. And since Montreal is an island, I'd have to show him some bridges. Probably the Jacques Cartier, to see the view of the St. Lawrence. It's prettier in summer, of course. In the winter I'd take him at night, to see all the lights."

Just as Jennie was becoming enthusiastic about this imaginary tour, the phone rang and Wes lifted the receiver. "Adler here," he said.

Jennie recognized Blanche Laure's dramatic voice. It had a vibrato, like a singer, and this time it sounded sulky. "Darling, can you come right away? I *hate* this arrangement, being miles away from you."

"Yes, it's a damned nuisance," he said sympathetically.

"Can't you get your room changed?"

"I'll be there as soon as I can, Blanche. I'm busy right now." He hung up, frowning at the receiver. Blanche's demands always annoyed him, and it particularly angered him to act the lackey in front of this young woman. Of course he had to humor her.

Jennie bit her lip, wondering if she should admit what she'd overheard. Because it had just occurred to her that while there was no suitable room for Blanche on the fifth floor, the suite adjacent to hers on the top floor would soon be vacated.

"That was Ms. Laure," he said.

"I couldn't help overhearing, Wes," she said, and made her suggestion. "I don't know why I didn't think of it sooner. Mr. Benson had stressed that you all wanted to be together. The suite is occupied at the moment, but— maybe I could arrange a transfer once it becomes available."

"Would that be difficult?"

"If I used Ms. Laure's name..." she said, thinking aloud. To her considerable surprise, he drew his dark brows together in a scowl. This was odd, since he'd already suggested that device himself earlier.

"Of course, if it were empty it would be ideal, but I wouldn't dream of disturbing your other clients. We've been enough bother already. It was kind of you to mention it. I believe I can wait until the client leaves. I'd better go and see what Blanche wants. The star, you know," he explained.

The mistress, Jennie thought, was more like it. She went below and checked the reservations book. The couple in the suite next to Blanche's were checking out in two days. She'd tell Wes he could move in. He wasn't so bad, really. Not as demanding as Blanche and not as silly as R.K.

Benson. But she didn't care much for the way he catered
to his *star*. She began the nearly impossible chore of trying
to cadge tickets for *Mother Courage*. Her contact at the
box office, Alfred Ouimet, was adamant. There were no
tickets, period.

Jennie refused to accept defeat. She knew there were
always a few good seats kept on reserve. On her noon
hour she went to the theater to beg in person. No tickets.
She accosted the scalpers. The price had risen to one
hundred dollars a seat, which made her blood boil. Finding no recourse, she returned to the box office and
conceded defeat.

"Mr. Adler, of Olympia Films, wants to know if it's
possible to get a pair of tickets for himself and Blanche
Laure for tomorrow night," she said. It angered her to
have to use his name, but the two hundred dollar price tag
angered her more. She felt it was important to find the
best deal for the hotel's customers.

"Blanche Laure! No kidding!" The clerk's eyes
popped. "How do I know they're for her and Adler?"

"Oh come off it, Alfred," she scolded. "You know
perfectly well she's staying at the Mont Royal. Why would
I lie to you and jeopardize getting tickets in future? You'll
see her for yourself, tomorrow night."

"Well, all right, I'll give you the set we save for celebrities. If you had told me who they were for, I could have
saved you a trip," he said reasonably.

Why hadn't she? What insanity had made her want to
get those tickets without using Mr. Adler or Ms Laure as
clout? After all, this wasn't a contest. She was merely
providing a service. She got the tickets and went back to
the hotel, still chastising herself for being an idiot.

R.K. Benson was waiting outside her door. His coat and
hat were draped across his lap. He wore a light jacket,

with the sleeves pushed up, and an open-necked silk sports shirt. Jennie was surprised he wasn't drenched in gold chains, but he only wore one very fine one with a diamond inset. The outfit would have been just right for Miami. In the middle of a Canadian winter, it looked foolish.

"We have a lee-tle problem, J.M.," he smiled.

"That's what I'm here for. Let's hear it."

"Rightie-ho. It's Ruby."

"She didn't like her steak?"

"Loved it. Super, no trouble there. Our congrats to the chef."

Jennie didn't think Pierre would appreciate "congrats" from a pooch. "Does she need a shrink, R.K.? Having a nervous spell?" she asked.

"No, but the rest of us will if Blanche doesn't settle down. She's preparing a fit of hysterics, I think, because of not having Wes beside her."

"I can take care of that soon, if she can do without him for a few nights," Jennie said ironically. "So what's the problem with Ruby?"

"It's—" He blushed. At least, she thought he blushed beneath his golden tan. "It's a matter of toilet training— the lack thereof, actually."

"She's wet the Aubusson!" Jennie exclaimed in horror.

"Puddles all over the room. You wouldn't think such a small dog... Of course, Blanche sometimes feeds her champagne. It's beginning to smell, J.M. You'll handle it?"

"You bet I'll handle it!" Jennie said through gritted teeth.

She marched into Mr. Simon's office. "We'll have to change Blanche Laure's carpet. The dog is wrecking them."

"You should have done that before her arrival," he said, without looking up from his papers.

"You told me not to!"

He didn't deny it. In fact, his refusal to meet her eyes was as good as an admission. "Do it when Ms. Laure is out," he said. "We don't want to offend her by asking her to stand in the hall while we shift furniture about. Take the less valuable carpets from storage and substitute them. You'll have to send the Aubusson out for cleaning."

"I'll put it on Mr. Adler's bill," she said grimly.

Mr. Simon looked up then. "Do you suppose Ms. Laure would like us to keep the dog for her? You could keep it in your office, Ms. Longman. I'm sure she'd be glad to get rid of it. It yaps incessantly."

"I don't want it in my office! And, anyway, she treats it like a child. She wouldn't part with it."

There was a noise in the hallways that sent Mr. Simon rushing to his door. He was just in time to see Blanche sweeping down the hall, Ruby in the crook of her arm, and her entourage following after her.

He dashed out and said, "Can I be of help, Ms. Laure?"

"I'll need a masseur's table in my room. And the hair-dressing facilities are entirely insufficient. In despair, I'm going to the *public* hairdresser for a shampoo," she said accusingly.

"But we have a beauty parlor in the hotel, Ms. Laure."

"Jacques, my coiffeur, will have to use those facilities. If you hope to cater to an international clientele, Mr. Simpson, I suggest you equip your rooms adequately." She strode angrily away.

"That's Simon," he said weakly.

Blanche had already walked away. Her hairdresser, a snooty-looking man with his own black hair pulled back in a ponytail, gave a sniff and darted to catch up with her.

"Get her what she needs, Ms. Longman," Mr. Simon said with an air of authority and returned to his office.

What Blanche needed, Jennie thought, was a good shaking. But she asked the housekeeping staff to send up a beauty parlor chair for Ms. Laure. She would have done it earlier if Jacques had requested it. Did they think there was space, in even a large suite, for all the equipment anyone might possibly want? She ordered the massage table, too. While Blanche was busy, Jennie slipped upstairs to view the damage done to the carpet, and wait for the arrival of the ordered items.

The beautiful suite looked as if someone was holding a rummage sale. Luggage and gowns and shoes were tossed all over. Blanche needed a maid more than she needed a hairdresser or masseur.

The carpet appeared to be salvageable. Jennie thought if she could send it out to the cleaners very soon, it could probably be refurbished. The trouble was not knowing how long Blanche would be occupied. There would be another scene if she returned to find her furniture in the hall. While Jennie stood looking at the stains, frowning and thinking, there was a light tap on the door. Without waiting for an answer, the door opened and Wes Adler strolled in.

After his shower, he had put on a bulky sweater and jeans. Both fit admirably, showing the outlines of his well-muscled body without pinching it. He glanced down at the soiled carpet and with a wicked grin he said, "Shame on you, Ms. Longman."

In her bad mood, Jennie was annoyed at the joke. "You're right. I should have had the carpets changed before she came."

Wes examined the carpet. "R.K. should have warned you. The last Persian carpet I had to replace set me back two thousand. I hope this one isn't totally destroyed."

"I think it can be restored, but I have to remove it right away, before those stains set."

"No time like the present. Where's Blanche?"

"At the hairdresser, but I don't know how long she'll be."

"How long do you need?" he asked.

"Half an hour would do it," she said hopefully. "Could you make sure she doesn't come back?"

"Blanche's hair never takes less than an hour. Can I give you a hand?"

Jennie stared in amazement. "The staff will do it. I'll call them right now."

She expected Wes to take his leave. Instead, he came into the room and waited while she made the arrangements. They chatted about the weather and other safe subjects till the hotel workers came to change the carpet. The new replacement didn't cover the entire floor, but the end of the carved bed had to be lifted to remove the original. Jennie could hardly believe her eyes when Wes took one end of the bed to help the workmen lift it. He wasn't awkward about it, either—he knew how to use his legs and back, rather than just his arms.

He noticed her surprise and decided to goad her. "Am I breaking some union rules?" he joked. "Maybe directors aren't allowed to move furniture."

"We won't tell," one of the workmen laughed.

"Don't strain your back," Jennie said.

"I'm flattered at your concern."

"Personal liability claims are expensive," she said briskly.

"You're all heart, lady. You can pay me from the money you'll make on my bill."

"This will only be a cleaning bill, I hope."

He came and joined her. "And the Sèvres vase—or dare I hope it was an imitation?"

"There are no imitations at the Mont Royal," Jennie said, with an imperious glance worthy of Blanche Laure.

Wes was becoming intrigued by this woman, who refused to be impressed by his star status. It was unnatural. He'd step up his charm tactics. "Too bad—these damages will end up costing me a fortune. But I can still afford to take you out to dinner," he said, waiting for her reaction.

Jennie completely ignored the implied invitation. "I got your reservations at Les Copains, ringside."

He swallowed his surprise and said, "Good. And will I be seeing *Mother Courage* tomorrow night?"

"Yes, I arranged that, too."

"You *are* efficient."

There was another tap at the door. The workmen deposited the massage table, then the hairdresser's chair.

"Where the devil are you going to put all that stuff?" Wes exclaimed.

"You should have got your star a double suite. She requested these items," Jennie replied crossly.

Wes hunched his shoulders and grinned. "Hey, don't take your bad humor out on me. We were speaking about dinner one evening..."

"I don't date clients, Mr. Adler. Hotel policy," she added untruthfully. The policy was her own, but she still thought it was a good one. Making friends with the customers could cause trouble, and this particular set of customers were trouble enough already.

"Does that mean I have to take my business to the Ritz?" he joked.

"That's up to you, but I don't date strangers, either."

He was astonished at her blunt answer. "We're not strangers. We're acquaintances. Until a minute ago we were on a first name basis. I'm Wes, remember?"

Jennie bustled about, rearranging the room. She felt acutely uncomfortable with Mr. Adler's gray eyes examining her in that flirtatious way. It wasn't the first time she'd been approached by a client. It was always uncomfortable, but she could handle it. What really irked her was that he was already having an affair with Blanche.

To remind him of that fact, she said, "Will you and Ms. Laure be dining at the hotel this evening before you go out?"

"I'd like a table for twelve, at eight. You are aware of Blanche's rather unique dietary requirements?"

"Mr. Benson explained them to me. That's all taken care of."

"Good. I'll try to talk her out of taking the dog with her."

Jennie was relieved that she had the law to back her up on this one. "Unfortunately, the city doesn't allow dogs in public dining rooms, Mr. Adler. No exceptions, not even for movie stars."

"Unfortunately?" he asked. "I'd say thank goodness."

"I'd appreciate it if you could see that Ms. Laure lays newspapers on the floor for Ruby before she leaves. These carpets are valuable."

"I'll lock her in the bathroom—the dog, I mean. Or are the tiles valuable, too?" He smiled.

"As a matter of fact, they are. They were imported from a castle in Portugal, but they're waterproof," she said, and turned to leave.

Wes cocked his head to one side and watched her retreat. He admired her trim ankles and swaying form. "Jennie!" he called.

She stopped at the door and looked over her shoulder. He read the impatience in her flashing green eyes, but pressed on, "If dinner is out, how about lunch some day?"

She shook her head. "Don't be difficult, Mr. Adler."

"If you say so. Anything to oblige. Will it be okay if I'm impossible?"

Jennie just shook her head and left. She didn't allow herself to smile until she was safely in the elevator, going back to her office. These movie people were really different. Why would a famous movie director try to date her, when it was clear that he was seeing Blanche Laure? If he wanted variety in his love life, he could probably have his pick of eager starlets.

Wes Adler waited till the elevator had left, then he softly locked Blanche's door and escaped to his own room. As he returned to his quarters, he was smiling. Jennie Longman was doing a good job of deflating his ego. A man in his position, who had been courted by dozens of beautiful women, was apt to get a bloated idea of his own irresistibility. Of course it was just a matter of time. All beautiful women wanted to be movie actresses. With that lure dangling in front of Jennie's eyes, she'd soon give in.

He'd make it perfectly clear he wasn't looking for a new leading lady. He didn't want to mess up the life of a nice kid like Jennie, but a man did need female companionship. Wes didn't think of Blanche as a woman. She was something intangible—she was a star, which was quite different.

Chapter Three

I know it's an imposition, Ms. Longman," Mr. Simon said, "but this is Ms. Laure's first meal at the hotel, and I would really appreciate it if you would stay around until it's over. Or at least well underway."

Jennie had nothing special planned for the evening, so she agreed. In fact, she looked forward to it. The Mont Royal was an interesting place to be at this particular time. The dining room was booked solid with clients hoping to see Blanche Laure. She went to the kitchen to discuss with Pierre the various cooking details R.K. Benson had given her.

Entering Pierre's kitchen was always a pleasure. She liked the noise and confusion of half a dozen cooks clattering pans, chopping and sautéing, clad in white hats, bending almost in unison over their work. The steam and sizzle always made her hungry. The aromas wafting around that evening were mouth-watering. She inhaled herbs and roasting meats, intermingled with the tantalizing smell of a caramel sauce in the making. A tray of escargots, drizzled with butter and champagne, was ready to slip into the oven. A side of beef was turning slowly on the rotisserie, and the sous-chef was just grating cheese on top of a tray of coquilles St. Jacques.

But it was mainly Ms. Laure's vegetarianism that concerned Pierre. "I've prepared this special ratatouille for her," he said. "Will you try it, Jennie? It's difficult getting a hearty flavor into a vegetable dish without meat or even a meat stock, but I think the wine helps."

Jennie tasted it and nodded. Not being a vegetarian herself, she found the dish a little bland, but to Ms. Laure it would probably be delightful. The herbs and wine lent a delicate aroma. "It's delicious," she said.

"I plan to serve it *en casserole*, with melted cheese on top," Pierre explained.

"That'll be the finishing touch," Jennie said. "Why don't you call it Ratatouille Blanche? That might please her."

"Yes, except blanche means white, and the dish is so colorful. I thought, perhaps, Ratatouille à la Laure."

"Even better."

"Will you be eating in the dining room, or shall I send dinner to your office?" Pierre asked.

"I'd better stay in my office. The Contessa Lisurga isn't feeling well. The doctor is with her now. I might have to make arrangements for her to go to the hospital, and she'll have orders for me before she leaves. She's here on business, so there'll be people to notify. I'll have one of those steaks broiled over mesquite, please."

Pierre gave her a scoffing look. Being a very French chef, he preferred his steaks cooked in the pan.

"Just to try it," she smiled. "I'm sure it won't come close to the way you prefer to prepare it."

"Ah *oui*. For *you* it is a novelty. *Je comprends*. Why do people come to a foreign country wanting their food the same as at home? *Provincials!* When do you want dinner?"

"In about half an hour, or whenever you can find time."

Jennie kept her door ajar to watch for celebrities entering the dining room. Blanche wore white that evening. She found it showed up well in darkened rooms and allowed her fans to spot her more easily. After her trip to the hairdresser and her visit from the masseur, she glowed from head to toe. Her throaty voice wafted along the corridor.

"And when de Gaulle pinned on the *Légion d'honneur*, he said, 'Mam'selle Laure, this is the finest bosom I have ever decorated.' Of course his English was unsteady, but really!"

"I would have to agree with de Gaulle," R.K. Benson chimed in dutifully. He was on one side of Blanche, Wes on the other.

Jennie noticed Wes had changed into a dark suit for the evening. Not formal, but a business suit with white shirt and tie. He smiled down at Blanche, murmuring something Jennie couldn't hear. Another compliment on her bosom, no doubt. Mr. Simon rushed forward to usher them into the dining room, in case they lost their way along the perfectly straight corridor.

Jennie closed her door and went on with her paperwork. In five minutes, there was a call from the contessa's suite asking for an ambulance. The next fifteen minutes were hectic. Jennie made the call, then rushed upstairs to see what she could do for the contessa. She came down with a list of phone calls to make, notifying relatives and business associates. Fortunately she had managed to get the names of a few people who spoke English.

She phoned Mr. Simon to tell him. "Not ptomaine poisoning, I hope!" he exclaimed.

"Nothing to do with the hotel, P.S.," Jennie assured him. "It's a chronic ailment. The contessa wants her room kept. She hopes to be back in two days."

Jennie was on the phone to Italy when her door opened. Mr. Simon came bustling in, his face red, his eyes wild. "She hates it! She called it bland pap! Pierre is threatening to quit—we've got to do something, Ms. Longman."

"Who hates what?" Jennie exclaimed.

"Ms. Laure. She sent back her dinner. She said if we *dare* to call that disastrous dish after her, she'll sue! Then she ripped up the menu."

While Simon was babbling incoherently, Wes appeared in the doorway behind him. "Good evening, Mr. Simon," he smiled. "May I have a word with your concierge?"

"I was just telling her," Mr. Simon said.

"I tasted the ratatouille myself," Jennie said earnestly. "It wasn't exactly piquant, but what can you expect without meat?"

Wes blinked in surprise. "Without meat! Good God, no wonder it tasted like vegetable soup."

"But she's a vegetarian!" Mr. Simon reminded him.

"Ah, did R.K. not tell you?" Wes said calmly. "Blanche is a vegetarian who likes meat, preferably red meat."

"But does she *eat* it?" Jennie asked in confusion.

"Avidly, as long as it's disguised as something else."

"Oh, lord," Jennie moaned. "Pierre didn't even use meat stock for flavoring. But how can meat be disguised as anything else?" Improvisation failed her.

"By camouflage," Wes explained. "Cut in very small pieces, sautéd till tender, it passes as mushrooms, or some esoteric vegetable. And, of course, a good stock is used generously to impart flavor."

"R.K. might have told me!" Jennie said. "Has Blanche left or is there still time to..."

"There's time," Wes said calmly. "I ordered her a bottle of Dom Pérignon and got her started on her *Smile of the Tiger* story. It involves the film made in India, during which the great white hunter hired as technical advisor fell madly in love with her. The inevitable fate of all who cross her path. The story takes fifteen minutes. Shall we go to the kitchen?"

Mr. Simon stared in astonishment. "I assure you, Mr. Alder, it isn't necessary for you to..."

"I'll oversee the preparation of the—er, Montreal mushrooms." Wes smiled. He offered Jennie his hand and helped her from her chair.

"I'm in the midst of making very important phone calls," she said uncertainly. "The contessa—" She looked from Mr. Simon to Wes, unsure which job was more urgent.

Wes took the list from her desk, then handed it to Mr. Simon. "Would you be so kind, Mr. Simon?"

"Certainly." He took the list and looked at it.

"I'm down to number three," Jennie said.

Wes took her hand and they darted out of the office, down to Pierre's kitchen. The chef was in despair. If he had had any hair, he would have been pulling it, but his scalp was as smooth as an egg.

"*Je ne comprends pas! C'est impossible!* The recipe was from *Escoffier*, with a few additions of my own," Pierre explained. "I used the very best champagne in my coquilles. How could she not like it? Was there too much garlic?'' he demanded. His forehead was beaded with moisture. Such a catastrophe had never before struck him.

Wes said gently, ''Don't disturb yourself, Pierre. Your cooking is exquisite. I've never tasted such coquilles St. Jacques.''

''But the ratatouille!''

''We are going to add some mushrooms,'' Wes explained. He glanced around the kitchen. ''From that side of beef, I think. Thinly slivered, and with some pan juices for the sauce . . .''

Pierre stared in horror. ''Yes, I know,'' Wes continued in a flat tone, ''Ms. Laure perpetuates the fiction that she's a vegetarian, but what her public doesn't know has never hurt her so far.''

Once Pierre understood the situation, he sliced off a piece of tenderloin, shaving it into paper-thin slices. The sharp knife flew through the air in a way that seemed to threaten his fingers. He spooned the pan gravy and meat into the casserole. He tasted it, then offered a spoonful to Wes. ''*Ah, c'est bon, ça!*'' he said, smacking his lips.

Wes tried it and said, ''*Magnifique!* You'll find all is forgiven, Pierre. I hope I find the same?'' he asked, with a disarming smile. ''I'm terribly sorry we've been such a nuisance.

''*Oh, Monsieur, pas du tout*. You have saved the day! My reputation—''

Jennie stood back, watching the incident. It showed a thoughtful side of Wes Adler she hadn't expected. He didn't have to go so far out of his way to smooth Pierre's ruffled feathers. It also confirmed her opinion of Blanche Laure. Why couldn't she have eaten her meal and kept quiet, like a civilized person? What was even harder to understand was why Wes bothered with such an egotist. Blanche was pretty, but she was quite a bit older than Wes.

And, really, the way he spoke of her hardly sounded as though he loved her. The film was finished, so that couldn't be why he had to cater to her.

As they left the kitchen, Jennie said, "Why does Ms. Laure insist on calling herself a vegetarian? There's no special virtue in it."

He looked down, putting his hand on her elbow. After this shared incident, he thought Jennie might relent and go out with him. She was really very attractive, and what interested him even more was her reserve. "It's a long story. Why don't I tell you over lunch tomorrow?" he suggested.

Jennie gave him a weary look. "Because we won't be having lunch together tomorrow."

He grinned. "The next day's good for me." This one was a tough nut to crack, but the more she refused, the more determined he became to ask her out. "But you won't want to wait to hear the long story. If you'll tell me where you're having lunch tomorrow, I'll phone and relate the story while you eat. It's rather an interesting one, actually," he tempted.

"Not to me, it isn't. It was just a passing thought."

"I've just had one of those myself—passing thoughts, I mean. We're all going to Les Copains after dinner. It wouldn't be a date, exactly, if you joined us." He looked for signs of weakening, and was surprised to see her chin firm mutinously.

"No, it certainly wouldn't, since you're accompanying Ms. Laure."

"There are eight men to four women. You would have an ample number of escorts to choose from."

"All of them clients of the hotel," she reminded him.

"And all of them strangers—except me. Now that I've let you in on the deep, dark secret of Ms. Laure's 'vegetarianism,' surely we're friends. I don't trade secrets with just anyone, you know."

"You can count on my discretion, Mr. Adler. I won't tell a soul."

It appeared to Wes that she hadn't picked up on that intimation of exclusiveness. What was it going to take to get her interested? "Perhaps you'd better slip the word to the other hotel chefs," he said. They approached the hallway and stopped. Wes still held her elbow, reluctant to leave.

"You'd better get back to Ms. Laure," she said.

He glanced at his watch. "No hurry. The great white hunter is just showing her how to hold a rifle. In about forty seconds, a white tiger will charge from the bush. Blanche will shoot it, and suffer lifelong remorse. But she is awarded the skin. There, you've weaseled the best part of the story out of me, you conniving woman. See you tomorrow," he said and left, dissatisfied with the meeting.

Jennie returned to her office and waited for Mr. Simon. He finally came in to tell her Ms. Laure had approved of her modified dinner. Simon had made the phone calls for the contessa. It was late, and another crisis had been resolved successfully. During the confusion Jennie had missed her dinner, but she didn't want to wait. She left and drove home, thinking of her busy day.

It wasn't until she was alone in her apartment that she thought of Wes. It would have been fun to go to Les Copains with the Hollywood contingent. They'd have all kinds of interesting stories to share. It was always intriguing to meet new people from another country, who were involved in such interesting work. If R.K. Benson, for instance, had asked her, she might have gone.

Now why would she have accepted his invitation? She really thought he was quite silly. Wes was much more interesting. Maybe too interesting. He was the kind of man she could become serious about. And why become serious about someone who was only going to be in town for a week? She went to the kitchen to scramble some eggs, although her thoughts wandered to that steak she had never gotten a chance to eat.

Morning wasn't the busiest time at the hotel, and after working late the night before, Jennie didn't go in until ten o'clock the next day.

"There's a note on your desk from Adler," Mr. Simon told her. Jennie felt a surge of emotion, but remained calm on the surface. Now what did Wes want? Was it to ask her out for lunch again?

"Oh, the contessa is back," Mr. Simon added. "It was just an attack of indigestion. She wants a taxi for a private tour of the city at two this afternoon."

"Fine, anything else?" Jennie asked.

"I have a representative from a psychiatrists' association coming at eleven to see about using the hotel for a convention in June. It's smallish, about fifty heads. You might check our reservations to see if we can work them in. It's early June, so we might manage it. Psychiatrists shouldn't be too troublesome," he added thoughtfully.

"Unlike movie actors, huh?" Jennie asked archly.

"I was a little disappointed in Ms. Laure," he admitted. "It shows a lack of breeding, don't you think, to make such a fuss over nothing?"

"I agree."

"It's all a sham with that crowd. Surface glitter, but underneath they're crude and common. Very good for business, of course. We'll have to do all we can to make their stay pleasant. You'd better see what Adler wants," he said. He pointed to the sealed envelope on her desk, then left.

Jennie opened it reluctantly. The note, scribbled on hotel stationery, said:

> I'm off to Brother André's shrine to seek repentance for my sins. I'll need three decorative young ladies for a party tomorrow evening at eight. And now that you and I are old friends, dare I hope? I'm sure you can oblige me with the first request, at least. You might try the modeling agencies. They should have some pretty faces.
>
> Wes.

According to the itinerary, Olympia Films didn't have a party booked for eight tomorrow. Her hand trembled and her head throbbed. "Three decorative young ladies." And last night he had said "There are eight men and only four women." Did he intend her to be the fourth? What he was asking her to do was get women for his crew—and possibly himself—and she was in the extremely unpleasant position of having to ask him why. Of course, she could just refuse outright. Women for a party—party girls. You didn't have to be a genius to read between the lines. And he included her, right in with the rest of them. Her blood simmered every time she thought of it.

The letter lent a bad flavor to Jennie's day. She checked the master calendar. Olympia wasn't scheduled for any social functions the next evening. So perhaps they were planning to have a party in their rooms. She'd heard enough about Hollywood parties to know the Mont Royal wouldn't tolerate such a thing. No, she couldn't risk it.

Mr. Simon had impressed upon her the importance of obliging the group, though, so she decided to check with him to make certain she was doing the right thing. "We're not in the escort business," he scoffed. "There'll be rock music blaring, drugs—and probably the police coming to break it up. I won't subject our guests, or our reputation to that sort of thing. Tell Mr. Adler we don't provide that service."

Jennie nodded in approval. "Very well, P.S."

"I'd appreciate it if you'd call me Mr. Simon, Ms. Longman. I'm not an actor."

Jennie was curious about her boss's bad mood. For him, the pleasure of the visit had centered around Blanche Laure. Blanche had lost part of her luster last night, but she wondered if anything had happened after she left.

"They're a difficult bunch," she said, hinting to hear more.

"They certainly are! And if she thinks we're going to put up with that ugly dog, she has another think coming. The wretch got loose this morning and created havoc with that lovely potted palm in the lobby. It frightened the life out of old Mrs. Whitcombe. She says Ruby bit her, but I couldn't locate any mark. She *did* put a hole in the woman's stocking. You'll have to buy her a new pair, Ms. Longman, and go up and pacify her."

"I'll take care of it. How did the dog get loose?" Jennie asked. "Did Ms. Laure bring it down to breakfast?"

"She ate in her room. An omelette of Montreal mushrooms," he added satirically. "She says the waiter left the door ajar, I took a bite out of his ear, but he says he closed the door tight, and I believe him. She came down here in her nightie, and hadn't the decency to apologize to Mrs. Whitcombe. Honestly, you have to wonder where she was reared."

All in all, it was shaping up to be a bad day. Jennie got the nylons and pacified Mrs. Whitcombe. The lady decided the skin on her leg hadn't been broken after all, though she mentioned her shattered nerves and dropped a hint of suing. This wealthy dowager was one of their regular clients. She was not at all amused to see movie stars running around in their nightgowns at her hotel.

"If we wanted to mix with *that* sort, we wouldn't come to the Mont Royal. Next time I shall try the Ritz," she said angrily.

"They're only staying a week. Why don't you give us another try?" Jennie suggested.

"Hmph. You would think Ms. Laure would have apologized at least. My son would like to have her autograph," she added. "He has always been a fan. I doubt he will continue to be one after today."

Jennie concluded that a visit or even a phone call from Ms. Laure would go a long way toward soothing the dowager's feathers, and determined that she'd try to arrange it. Personally, she thought it was about as likely as snow in July, but she'd try. Perhaps a hint of a possible lawsuit… She phoned Ms. Laure, but her hairdresser said she was under the dryer and couldn't be disturbed.

At noon hour, Jennie was tidying her desk to leave for lunch when there was a tap at her door. She answered it and looked up to find Wes standing there, wearing his navy pea jacket again, looking like a sailor. The wind had turned his cheeks red, and he was rubbing his arms to get warm. What flashed through her mind was that he didn't look like a lecher, especially when he smiled.

"Hi, Jennie. Did you get my note?" he asked, stepping in.

"Yes, I've been—thinking about it."

Now why was she frowning, and looking at him as if he'd grown another head? "There's no problem, I hope?" he asked.

His attitude struck her as arrogant, and she stiffened in response. "There is, actually."

He arched a black brow. "Solving guests' problems is your department, isn't it?"

"That depends on the problem. We don't supply party girls. We're a hotel, not a—a bordello," she said in confusion. Her cheeks felt hot, and Wes's diabolic grin didn't help any.

His grin hid a burning sense of anger. So that's what she thought of him! Why did people always assume anyone associated with the movie business was immoral? He came forward perching himself on the edge of her desk. With his face just inches from hers, he said, "My, my, what an active imagination you have."

"It doesn't take much imagination to figure out what you want those women for."

"I need escorts for my crew," he said flatly.

"Yes, for a party. I hope you aren't planning to hold one of your wild Hollywood parties here."

"No, we find the atmosphere here a little chilly. Our wild party is planned elsewhere."

"Well you can plan to get your women elsewhere, too. We're not in the business of soliciting."

His anger gelled, and when he spoke, his voice was hard. "I should hope not! This is *supposed* to be a classy joint. At the prices you charge, it should be."

"We'll be lucky if we break even on your visit!" she snapped.

"You're damned poor managers if you don't," he riposted. "So you cannot arrange to provide escorts for my men?"

"Cannot is the wrong word, Mr. Adler. We will not. There are plenty of escort agencies in the yellow pages. You shouldn't have any trouble."

He was going to enjoy putting this young lady in her place. Why was it that the pious people always had the worst imaginations? "I never do. The dates are for my crew. *I'll* be escorting Blanche."

She was angry. But the thought of him consorting with Blanche added fuel to the fire. "Maybe you could use your influence with Ms. Laure to get her to apologize to Mrs. Whitcombe," she said stiffly.

The name was new to him. "Who is Mrs. Whitcombe, and how did Blanche offend her? Or was just being an actress offense enough?"

"She's the hotel guest Ruby attacked this morning. I'd appreciate it if you could get Ms. Laure to keep that mutt out of the lobby."

That damned dog! Why couldn't Blanche keep it on a leash? But to think of that little runt, not weighing ten pounds, hurting anyone was ridiculous. His expression wasn't far from cynical. "Attacked by a raging chihuahua, was she? I hope the lady survived. Ruby barks. She doesn't bite."

"She tore Mrs. Whitcombe's stockings. She's an elderly widow—she was very shaken up."

Wes's brows drew together in a quick frown. "I'll speak to Blanche," he said curtly.

"I'd appreciate it. It might prevent a lawsuit. The hotel is responsible for its guests' well-being."

"Not for all its guests, it seems."

She lifted an eyebrow and said, "Meaning?"

"Meaning my crew."

"We're looking after them."

"Not their social needs," he taunted.

"We draw the line there."

Wes rose from the desk and looked down on her from his superior height. "The Minister of Culture would be surprised to hear his grand ball described as a wild Hollywood party. He sent us eight courtesy tickets. Of course, it's really Blanche they want, but three bachelors are filling in the other seats. They don't know any ladies in town, and you don't go to a ball without a date." That shook her.

Jennie stared in consternation. She had just insulted a very important client. The minister's annual dinner and ball was a prestigious affair. If Mr. Simon had known this, he would have bent over backwards to supply escorts. She felt foolish; worse, she felt guilty. A flush crept up her neck and stained her cheeks. She looked down, and when she lifted her eyes she saw that Wes was gazing at her intently. He wasn't smiling or laughing at her. In fact, his eyes blazed angrily. In about two seconds, he was going to tell her he was leaving the hotel and storm out.

"I apologize," she said, in a breathless voice. "I just assumed—"

"That's a dangerous thing to do. Don't worry about it. I won't tell the boss on you."

"Then you're not leaving?" she asked hopefully.

He didn't answer the question directly. Other things were uppermost in his mind. "Did you really think I'd ask you to hire ladies of the evening for me?" he demanded.

Jennie's tongue flickered lightly over her lips, that had become dry from worry. Wes felt a stirring of emotion at the sight. It was an old starlet's trick, but he realized Jennie did it unconsciously.

"You wanted women for a party," she said. "You stressed that they should be pretty. What was I supposed to think?"

"I would have leaped to the conclusion that three bachelors, strangers in town, wanted presentable dates. But then, of course, I'm just a Hollywood rabble-rouser."

"I'll phone an escort agency," she said, hoping to make a peace offering.

"Forget it. They can get their own dates. Now what about this Mrs. Whitcombe? Neither of us wants a lawsuit or a scandal. Was she really hurt?"

"No, the skin wasn't broken. She was just upset."

"Then she'll be happy to settle out of court. How much do you think—"

"She isn't after *money*!" Jennie said, shocked at the idea.

"Everybody's after money."

"Don't be so cynical. A visit from Blanche would do it. I think she was offended because she never received an apology."

"I'll take care of it. You know, what never ceases to amaze me is that people have such a low idea of our moral standards in Hollywood, yet they're all dying to meet us. Why is that?"

He was taunting her, but Jennie thought about it a moment and realized it was true. "Maybe they just want a little brush with glamour," she said pensively.

"Not enough to get tainted, you mean?" he asked.

"Well, not enough to get involved or hurt."

"Getting involved doesn't lead inexorably to getting hurt. I know many happily married actors and directors and producers. Some of them even live in houses and have mortgages and children, like real people. They go to PTA meetings and eat ordinary food."

Jennie listened, and was struck by his earnestness. Why was he telling her all this? There seemed some message beneath the words. It made her nervous. To break the growing tension she said, "Not all that ordinary. I never met a vegetarian who ate meat before."

Wes shook his head ruefully. "Blanche is unique. She's not so bad when you get to know her. She's had a tough climb up the ladder and now that's she's on top she feels she deserves the best life has to offer. If you'd ever come down off your high horse and agree to go out with me, I could tell you all about her."

Jennie was tempted to accept, but now that she wanted to go there wasn't really much time. "You're going to the play with Blanche tonight and tomorrow night you are accompanying her to the Minister of Culture's ball."

"I'm not having lunch with her today," he pointed out, feeling the blood racing through his veins. It had been a long time since he'd worked so hard to get a woman's interest.

"I'm busy," she said, and hunched her shoulders as if it didn't matter to her.

"Is it an unbreakable date?"

"Heavy." She smiled. "We have Art Makepiece, the author, staying here. I'm setting up a lecture for him in the ballroom. I told him I'd make sure the seats were arranged, that the blurbs were available at the door, whether the P.A. system is working. I have to see that the coffee and doughnuts are on hand. You know, the responsibilities of a concierge."

"This is the first time I lost out to a plate of doughnuts." Wes frowned. "What's Mrs. Whitcombe's room number?"

"212. She's in her room now."

"Will you order a dozen roses for Blanche's room and send a blank card? I'll have her fill in an apology and take it to Mrs. Whitcombe."

"Will she do it?" Jennie asked doubtfully.

"She will if she knows what's good for her," he scowled, and left in a thoroughly disgruntled mood.

Jennie was dissatisfied, too, but she decided she was really relieved that her schedule made it impossible to go out with Wes Adler. He was proving to be enough of a distraction without her becoming personally involved with him. What was the point? She felt a little foolish about the escort episode. It was nice of him not to make a fuss over it. He was probably a very nice man.

Chapter Four

Each day at the Mont Royal brought its share of problems and strife, its victories and unexpected pleasures. The day had begun badly for Jennie, but the afternoon proved more enjoyable. Art Makepiece, the author, was charming. He gave Jennie a signed copy of *Ring of Fire*, his latest best-seller, for her help in arranging his lecture. That was the kind of gratuity she really appreciated, something personal.

Mrs. Whitcombe came into her office, gushing and waving a piece of paper, which proved on a closer look to be an autographed picture of the star.

"She signed it—Blanche Laure. So gracious! She came to my room in person and brought me flowers. I shall save one for my son. You won't mention to anyone what I said earlier, Miss Longman?" That was really the reason she had come to Jennie, to make sure Blanche Laure didn't learn that Mrs. Whitcombe had been, quite justifiably, angry with her.

"You won't be suing then?" Jennie asked with relief.

"Sue that sweet Blanche Laure?" Mrs. Whitcombe laughed at the very idea. "Whatever for? I wasn't even scratched. Just a tiny run in my stocking. Little Ruby is nervous in a strange place," she added, with the knowing nod of an insider.

Pierre was also glowing with pleasure when he showed Jennie the signed photograph Blanche Laure had sent him. He was going to have it framed and hung in his kitchen. The magic of stardom had worked its magic. Rude manners and selfishness were forgiven with a smile.

Jennie knew Wes was behind the flowers and apology to Mrs. Whitcombe and assumed he had told Blanche to send the picture to Pierre, as well. Left to her own devices, Blanche wouldn't have a fan left in the world, despite her great acting talent.

During a peaceful moment, Jennie was thumbing through *Ring of Fire* when there was a tap at the door. She hastily closed the book, in case it was Mr. Simon. "Come in," she called.

The door opened and R.K. Benson strutted in, minus the sunglasses today. He was decked in a powder blue cashmere sweater and black cords. "Hi, J.M. I hear congrats are in order."

"For what?" Jennie asked.

"I hear you tweaked Adler's nose. That takes a brave lady." He slouched on the chair by her desk and stretched his booted feet out in front of him.

"I certainly didn't intend to do that."

"I'm amazed that he was still smiling. You've worked a miracle." Jennie was a little surprised that Wes had told anyone about the incident. "No sweat. He likes straight-talking people. You were out of line, however. The chicks for tomorrow night are strictly window-dressing. What do you take us for, rock stars? Not that they're all sex fiends."

Jennie felt a need to defend and explain, and since R.K. was there she found herself apologizing to him. "I'm sorry if I offended anyone. It was a perfectly logical mistake."

"Tell me about it. We're show-biz, therefore we live on drugs and sex and seeing our name in lights. There's plenty of that in the industry, but Adler runs a tight ship."

Jennie began to wonder just why R.K. Benson had come to see her. "I'm glad to hear it," she said. "Is there something I can help you with, R.K.?"

"Adler delegated the date detail to me. You can help me choose an escort agency. I don't want to contact the wrong kind—you know what I mean?" He wiggled his eyebrows. "We want ladies."

"The Elite has a good reputation," she said.

"Great, I'll take the ball from here."

R.K. leaned back in his seat. "Do you wish to use my phone?" she asked.

"No, no. I just had an idea. I'll lay it on you, and you tell me what you think. Here's the scenario—you, me. We do the formal dinner bit, then cut out. You show me your town. I'll be happy to recip any time you find yourself in L.A. What do you say, J.M.?"

"I don't date clients, R.K. Hotel policy."

"Hey, who's going to know? I won't tell if you don't."

Jennie took a breath, while searching for a polite but firm way to refuse him, R.K. came up with his own explanation before she spoke. "I get it. The media. There'll be cameras. This gala will generate a lot of ink. I understand. It's a pity you have to miss the party, but you wouldn't want to lose your job." He looked around the room with an amused air. "I guess you actually like this scene, huh?"

"Very much."

He gave her a disbelieving look. "I might be able to find you a spot in the organization," he tempted. "Olympia Films. Wall-to-wall glamour and glitz, J.M. First-class travel, rubbing shoulders with the stars. I can wangle intro's to all the important people. Burt, Clint— they're all Olympia fans."

"I didn't realize you had that much influence with Mr. Adler," she said. Her tone implied doubt.

"More with Blanche, to tell the truth, and she is very close to Adler." He lifted two fingers, held tightly together, wiggling them. "She'll do what I ask, and he'll do what she asks. I'm actually Blanche's public relations man, but since she did *Orphan* with Adler, she managed to slip me onto his payroll. No moss growing under Blanche's feet. I do a bit of liaison work for Olympia, too."

"Thanks for the offer, R.K., but I'm happy here."

"Don't say no. Why close doors, when leaving them ajar doesn't even dent the budget?" He rose slowly, stretched and said, "I have to go up and see Blanche now. I'll start singing your praises."

Jennie didn't bother repeating her lack of interest. "You might as well take her these tickets for tonight. She and Mr. Adler are going to a play." She handed him the tickets for *Mother Courage.*

He looked at them and shook his head. "I wonder why Adler's so determined for Blanche to see this play. They've been having shouting matches about it all week. I can tell you right now, she'll hate it. No decent music, the costumes are awful, and the story's a downer. God, I hope he doesn't skip out and stick *me* as her escort. He likes Blanche to be seen at all the right places for publicity, but he shuns the spotlight himself.'' He put the tickets in his pocket and left.

Jennie's next visitor didn't bother to knock. Blanche Laure just threw open the door and strode in as if she owned the place. Jennie felt a trembling excitement, and waited to hear why she had come.

Blanche was dressed for the street, in a long black coat and high black boots. A crimson scarf was wound like a blanket around her shoulders. Large sunglasses hid the upper half of her face, but in the bright light of day the lines in her cheeks were quite visible. But she was still an impressive sight. She filled the room with her presence, as surely as her movies filled theaters. In Blanche's arm, Ruby yapped a welcome.

''Hush, darling,'' Blanche said, patting the dog's nose. She finally glanced at Jennie. ''I won't be needing these, dear,'' she said in her throaty voice, and drew out the tickets for *Mother Courage*. Ruby snapped at them and managed to get hold of the envelope. Blanche gave the dog a token tap on the head and retrieved them. ''She's so quick! Ruby is very intelligent. Bad Ruby.'' Her rebuke, accompanied by a low laugh, sounded more like praise. ''I understand these are in short supply. You shouldn't have trouble scalping them. Thank you, dear.''

Without waiting for a reply, Blanche turned and swooped out of the office, crooning to her pesky little partner. Jennie stood staring at the tickets, that had cost her her lunch hour and a ton of trouble. ''I will not scream,'' she told herself, and began rapidly counting to ten.

When she had settled down, Jennie realized that the rushing excitement in her veins had more to do with having actually talked to Blanche Laure than with her anger

over the tickets. She hadn't uttered a word of complaint.
Like Mrs. Whitcombe and Pierre, she was too thrilled at
having had an encounter with the fabulous Blanche
Laure. She knew that when her friends asked "What's
new," the first thing she'd say would be "I met Blanche
Laure." She felt a niggling regret that she hadn't gotten an
autograph.

Jennie fingered the tickets, trying to decide what to do
with them. She wouldn't mind using one herself and calling a friend. Alfie Ouimet would never believe her again,
and he was a contact she couldn't afford to alienate. She
had assured him the tickets were for Blanche and Mr.
Adler. But it was Wes who had been eager to see the play.

Jennie was beginning to think she might bend her own
rule and go with Wes, if Blanche didn't want to go. She
wondered if he knew Blanche had returned the tickets.
R.K. only gave them to her half an hour ago. Maybe Wes
didn't know.

She lifted the phone and asked for his room. The
switchboard told her Mr. Adler was at a meeting with his
staff, so she left an urgent message for him to contact her.
The sooner she got the ticket business settled, the better.
Other matters came up to distract Jennie. Art Makepiece
dropped in to tell her the lecture had gone well. There was
a call enquiring about reservations for a small convention the end of May, which would overlap slightly with the
psychiatrists' meeting in early June. She worked on the
logistics of that for a while and decided it couldn't be
done.

Jennie took her figures to Mr. Simon, and when she
returned to her office she found Wes waiting for her. She
was aware of a tightening in her chest at the sight of him.
A shock of black hair hung over his tanned forehead, and
in the bright light of day, she noticed his dove gray eyes

had an almost opalescent quality of shifting color. Since his meeting had been with his own staff, he hadn't bothered to dress in business clothes. His broad shoulders filled a navy V-necked sweater with a white T-shirt showing at the throat. It struck her as strange that the boss dressed so casually, while his employees dressed themselves like stars. But then the boss didn't have to try to make himself look important. He *was* important.

"You wanted to see me, Jen?" he asked.

"Come in," she said, and he followed her into her office.

"I was told it was urgent," he said, but the urgency didn't appear to cause him any alarm. His voice still had that languid, lazy sound. "I hope Blanche hasn't—"

"No, no." She smiled. "Maybe I used the wrong word. It's urgent, but not serious. This concerns the tickets for *Mother Courage*."

He touched his forehead. "I'm glad you reminded me, or I would have ended up at the theater without them. Do you have them handy?"

Jennie felt her heart sink. So Blanche hadn't told Wes she wasn't going. She'd have to tell him herself. She handed him the tickets. "I sent them to Blanche earlier and she gave them to me, saying she wasn't going. Do you want me to return them?"

"No way! I have to see the play, with or without her. I was hoping she'd come with me. I really wanted to take Blanche," he said, disappointed.

Jennie felt a heaviness in her chest that she didn't care to examine. She was beginning to think it was jealousy. "Try roses or champagne," she suggested with a smiling shrug.

"Roses are for minor favors. This one would need a diamond bracelet, at least."

Buying his way into Blanche's favor! Jennie gave him a disparaging look. "You know what it's worth to you," she said glibly. And she had balked at paying scalpers' prices for the tickets! She wished she had paid a hundred bucks each for them.

Wes didn't take any notice of Jennie's mood. "Did she sound really adamant?" he asked.

"Not particularly, but R.K. felt she wouldn't enjoy the play." She tossed her head in a show of indifference. "Why don't you take her someplace else?"

He gazed at her, a smile tugging at his lips. So Ms. Longman was beginning to feel pangs of jealousy, was she? This looked promising. "The point of the evening isn't to be alone with the Divine Blanche; it's to see Calvini's rendition of *Mother Courage. I'm* going, even if I have to—" He stopped mid-speech. Jennie hadn't tumbled for a party, but if she was reading Makepiece's latest opus she liked good literature and might like to see Bertolt Brecht. "I suppose you've seen the play?" he asked offhandedly.

She glanced up and he read the light of interest in her eyes. Wonderful eyes Jennie had, the whites so white and the green so green, with those mile-long lashes. "Not yet. The production has a limited engagement, and tickets are hard to come by," she said.

He opened the envelope and flipped the tickets enticingly. "Good seats," he said, glancing at her from the corner of his eyes. "I'll only be using one."

She waited, a smile beginning to hover at the corners of her lips. This was the perfect opening if he was going to ask her. Wes just went on flipping the tickets distractedly. "I can return the other," she said reluctantly.

He saw the growing interest and hesitated, planning his strategy. Let her think she wasn't going to get the offer; it might make her more enthusiastic. "A pity the hotel policy won't allow you to come with me." Was she going to break down?

She looked at him hopefully. "Yes," she said, but with no conviction. He hadn't let that stop him before.

"I'm a stickler for rules myself and I respect other companies' rules, too. Otherwise, I'd ask you to come with me," he said and smiled sadly, while biting back a grin. Time to change the subject.

He picked up Makepiece's novel and flipped through it. "I haven't had time to read this. Is it good?"

"I just got it this afternoon. Mr. Makepiece autographed it and gave it to me."

Those soft dove gray eyes could be extremely penetrating. Jennie felt as if he were looking through her. "The hotel *does* allow you to accept gifts from guests, does it?"

"Yes, certainly. It's a rule of thumb in the profession that if your tips don't exceed your salary, you aren't doing a good job."

He nodded. "Then I'll see you get tickets for the premiere of *Orphan*. It should be a good bash." Her smile was like a burst of sunshine. "Or would you be interested in attending a wild Hollywood party?" he challenged.

Jennie was disappointed he hadn't asked her to go to the play, but the premiere was even more exciting. "I've already apologized for my faulty assumption," she reminded him. "And since the party's here at the hotel, it can't be anything but top drawer. How come you're having it here, instead of in L.A.?"

"It's my way of saying thank you to the Quebec government. They were very helpful and gracious during the shoot. It seemed the polite thing to do."

"That was thoughtful of you!" she said, surprised.

His look was tinged with cynicism. "Yes, even *I* occasionally remember my manners. The tickets for the premiere are my thank you note to you."

Jennie realized she had unintentionally offended him, and said, "I'd love to go. I'll take Mr. Simon. You did say tickets—as in a pair?"

Wes stared in consternation. "Good lord! Are you and Simon an item? Is *that* why I haven't got to first base?"

"No! He's my boss!"

"That's right, and you said your boyfriend wasn't in town. Wouldn't you prefer to take *him* to the party? Or does he live too far away?"

Jennie's eyelids fluttered uncertainly. "I don't have a— I mean I'm not engaged or anything."

"That's a blow to my pride. I thought that must be why you were so determined not to break the hotel dating policies. Maybe there's hope for—" he hesitated a moment, then continued "—Simon yet. I'll see you get those tickets. Gotta run now." He waved and left.

Jennie sat frowning at the door, while her spirits sank. Now that he'd gone, she admitted that she was longing to see the play. And even more than that, she wanted to go out with Wes Adler. She wanted to be alone with him, to find out what he was really like. But she'd refused once too often. She didn't think Wes was the kind of man who would beg for a date.

At least the ticket business was settled. Alfie Ouimet might be satisfied with one celebrity. Of course, he'd be happier if it were Blanche. Everyone would recognize her, whereas Wes kept a lower profile. She wondered who Wes would ask to the play. He had a secretary, an older woman, a motherly type. Or would he take the pretty young press attaché who made no secret she was interested in him? The two other women in the group seemed to be attached to two of the men, one married and one going steady.

Finally, it was five-thirty, and the Olympia group hadn't planned anything special that evening, so Jennie decided to go home. Since she wouldn't be seeing the play, she would just stay home and start reading *Ring of Fire*. She might have a chance to discuss it with Mr. Makepiece tomorrow.

As she passed the desk, the clerk said, "Letter for you, Jennie," then handed her a sealed hotel envelope.

Jennie opened it before leaving, in case it was from a client, wanting something. She could see right away that the folded piece of paper only had a short note scrawled on it. She unfolded the paper and a single ticket for *Mother Courage* fell into her hand. Her heart quickened, and a smile curved her lips. She read the note.

Dear Jennie:
Enclosed is a small token of my appreciation for your help. Dates with customers, I know, are verboten, but I hope you are allowed to exchange a few words if you happen to meet them outside of the hotel.
                                        Hopefully, Wes.

Her footsteps flew over the marble floor of the lobby. The play started at eight, and she had to shower and change and do something to her hair.

The clerk lifted the phone and called Mr. Adler. "I'd say you're on, Mr. Adler. She was smiling from ear to ear, and flew out of here as if she were going to a coronation."

"Thanks, Ginnie."

"Any time. Shall I place that call to L.A. now?"

"Yes, please."

Mr. Adler sounded as though he were smiling from ear to ear too. Imagine, that lucky Jennie got a date with Wescott Adler!

Chapter Five

Jennie maneuvered her little red car through the chaotic Montreal traffic, east on Sherbrooke and up Côte des Neiges to her apartment building. It was a job that needed all her attention. The city had the reputation of having the wildest drivers in the country, and every time she drove Jennie realized how well deserved the reputation was.

Not wanting to waste time preparing supper, she settled for a ham on rye, while she thought about the evening. Meeting West at the show wasn't exactly a date, she rationalized. And, anyway, the ban on dating customers was her own invention. She'd drive her car and avoid the possible hassle of inviting him home for a drink after. Since she'd have to go on working with him, she didn't want to get deeply involved or establish hard feelings by having to refuse him.

Once that was settled, the next question was what to wear. Montreal women had the French flair for chic, and for an elegant evening at the theater, they'd be dressed to the nines. Dressing up was fun, and Jennie had plenty of fancy gowns she had worn when attending functions at work. As it was the dead of winter, she chose the fashionable warmth of a long-sleeved dress in white cashmere. The front, embroidered in gold leaves, didn't need any jewelry.

Her hair, loosed from its braid, surrounded her face in a springy halo. Deep tints of copper and gold gleamed in the lamplight as she brushed it. Her winter complexion needed a touch of rouge, and she added it sparingly. For evening, Jennie wore a silvery eye shadow and highlighted her eyes with feathery strokes of a pencil. The slightly feline tilt of her eyes stood out dramatically. She examined herself and decided to add big, dangly gold earrings, that would clink and tinkle every time she moved her head.

It was seven-thirty, and the show began at eight. Just time enough to drive to the Place des Arts theater and park. She should have expected to encounter a traffic delay. There was one when she reached downtown, and by the time she pulled into the parking lot, it was exactly eight o'clock. She hated arriving at the theater late and having to disturb the patrons, if the ushers let her in at all. When she checked her coat, the ushers were just closing the doors.

Jennie hurried, and got in just as the house lights dimmed. Since the usher was busy, she decided to find her own seat. The fading notes of the orchestra dulled to a hush as she went down the aisle, searching for her row. She knew the seats were on the aisle, and she spotted the empty one with no trouble. Wes had taken the aisle seat. He looked around at the sound of footsteps, and stood up when she stopped at his row.

For a moment he hardly recognized her. The business-like young lady with her hair pulled back had reverted to her proper style. She looked young, flushed and excited, and very lovely with that deep chestnut hair surrounding her little, gamine face.

In the fleeting glance Jennie managed while skimming past Wes, she noticed his look of surprise. Hadn't he expected her to come? She sat down and he turned to her.

"That's a relief!" he said in a low voice. "I didn't think you'd waste the ticket, but I wasn't sure you'd use it yourself. I was on the lookout for a uniform and French braid. Very nice." His glance flickered admiringly over her face.

His lazy voice held an undercurrent of excitement she hadn't heard before. That was the first thing Jennie noticed when she sat next to him, warming herself in the glow of his smile. His dove gray eyes had deepened to charcoal in the dim hall. The shoulder rubbing hers was covered by a dark jacket, and a sparkle of white shirt showed at the front. He was dressed in a business suit, but the feeling that swelled around her was far removed from anything so mundane. She felt as if she perched on the edge of some thundering excitement.

"I was afraid I wouldn't find you," she admitted, and heard a nervous laugh escape her lips.

He turned and smiled deeply into her eyes. "I'm delighted to hear you were looking. I've been here, waiting for you all along, Jennie." She read a deeper meaning beneath the words.

The shimmering gold curtains opened, sending a rush of anticipation through the audience. The couple in front of them didn't shush them, but they looked over their shoulders in an admonishing way. Obviously, conversation would have to wait till intermission. The show was serious without being heavy. There was some comedy and music of a rustic sort. Wes seemed completely absorbed in the drama throughout the first act.

When the curtain closed, he said, "Shall we move around and let the blood circulate?"

"I am a little stiff," she agreed.

His head inclined to hers and he gave her his hand to help her up. "Not nearly as stiff as you've been up to this evening," he said in his calm quiet way, which still carried an undertone of secondary meaning.

The crowded aisle slowed their exit. Walking behind Jennie, Wescott noted with approval the new hairstyle. There was a light, flowery scent wafting toward him. Her dress, clinging to svelte curves, looked soft and inviting. He had to work to control the impulse to run his hand along her body. It would be soft and warm and yielding beneath his fingers. Of course, he resisted. He knew by now that he couldn't hurry things with Jennie Longman.

"Something to drink?" he suggested.

"Coffee's fine. I'm a little thirsty."

There was a long line at the bar, so Jennie decided to go with him. "What changed your mind about meeting me?" he asked.

"I couldn't bear the idea of that expensive ticket going to waste. And I wanted to see the show."

He watched her with those peculiarly penetrating eyes. "And?"

"How many excuses do I need?"

"You don't need any excuses. I was waiting for the reason. Like you wanted to get to know me better, maybe," he suggested, and peered down to see her reaction.

"I was a little curious," she admitted.

"I'm underwhelmed by your enthusiasm." He had reached the head of the line and ordered two coffees. "Well, how are you liking me so far?" he asked, and grinned as he handed her one.

"Highly unsatisfactory, Mr. Adler. You forgot the sugar."

"Sugar! You mean sweetener. I haven't met a woman who would let real sugar near her cup in a dozen years. Not that I mean to suggest you have a weight problem." His eyes instinctively measured her curves. "Just right, I'd say."

"I only take one teaspoon," Jennie said, trying to ignore the way her body reacted to his appraisal.

He handed her a paper packet of sugar and they moved away from the crowded bar. "I'm glad you came, Jennie," he said. His mood was more serious than before. "I hope it won't jeopardize your job."

"No, it's my own rule not to date customers. And anyway, this isn't a date." But, of course, it was. What else could she call it? They were out together, and she was having a very good time. To add an air of business, she asked, "Did R.K. manage to get escorts for the men for tomorrow night?"

Wes studied her curiously for a moment before answering. "Is that what he was doing in your office? I wondered, when you mentioned this afternoon that you'd been speaking to him. I thought he was beating my time."

"That, too," she smiled, remembering that Benson had suggested she work for Olympia. "But did he get the dates?"

"Yes, and now let's not talk business any more tonight. I like the way you're wearing your hair. It looks very feminine, and sort of—preRaphaelite, if that's the

right school. I mean the artists who make women look like
saints."

"Saints!" she exclaimed, laughing.

The ludicrousness of his description occurred to him.
That wasn't what he meant, at all. "I meant a very sexy
saint." It was that halo of gleaming hair that brought the
word to mind. "Have I offended you?"

"That sounds like a contradiction in terms."

"Not at all. Wait till you see Blanche as the *Orphan*."

"I'm looking forward to it," she said eagerly. "I think
she is a wonderful actress."

Wes was a little surprised that she let the conversation
veer away from compliments to herself so quickly. It certainly wasn't the behavior of the actresses he'd known. "I
know the movie's good, and the premiere should be a
success. But, then, you already know that. You're in
charge of it. And now we're really not going to talk business any more. Tell me all about you."

She looked at the crowd, already beginning to drift
back into the hall. "In five minutes? My life hasn't been
an epic, but it would take longer than that."

He nodded. "You can tell me later, then. What I really
want to know is if you have any strenuous objections to
holding hands at the theater. Since they don't serve pop-
corn as they do at movies, I have a couple of hands that
don't know what to do with themselves."

She gave him a leery look. "You should have brought
your knitting," she said facetiously, and they returned to
the hall.

As soon as the curtain opened, he seized her hand and
held it for the rest of the show. It was cozy, sitting in the
dark with Wes. He hardly ever looked at her. She sensed
that he was completely absorbed in the drama, and soon
Jennie got caught up in the trials of *Mother Courage*, too.

During one of the production numbers, she let her mind wander a little. Wes seemed quite unaffected for an important director. But how would he behave on a second date? He certainly wasn't slow. Already his fingers were moving gently on hers, massaging them in a way that told her he enjoyed the intimacy of touching her. She enjoyed it, too.

When the play was over, they moved out with the throng. The surging crowd made it necessary to hold hands, to avoid being separated. "Where do we go for a nightcap?" Wes asked.

"Montreal has dozens of places. Do you want to go where there's music and people, or someplace conducive to conversation?"

"We've already done crowds. Let's go where we can talk and perhaps eat."

"There's a little after-theater bar just a block away. They serve oysters and steak-frites."

"Sounds good to me."

They went to get their coats. As he held Jennie's beaver coat for her he said, "Blanche wouldn't approve of this. She won't wear fur, at all. She's against cruelty to animals."

"Would she wear fur if it were disguised?" She smiled.

"That wouldn't serve the purpose. If fur doesn't look like fur, what's the point?"

Jennie shook her head. "If you lived in Montreal, you wouldn't ask. It's cold here, often below zero. And the wind from the St. Lawrence makes it worse."

He pulled the collar up around her neck, enjoying the sensuous luxury of the pile oozing between his fingers. His hand brushed her neck and Jennie said, to cover her confusion, "I'm afraid you'll be cold."

"I have you to keep me warm," he murmured in that lazy, languid way she was coming to know. The insinuation in his words made her feel as if a feather were tickling her spine, sending shivers along her nerve endings.

"It's only a few doors away," she said, and used buttoning her coat as an excuse to move away from him.

Even one block in the dead of winter was enough to make their ears tingle. They ran the last few yards, with Wes clinging to her arm, and were both happy to get out of the cold. La Maison d'Or was a dark, discreet *boîte* tucked in between a theater and a hotel. The muted strains of background music melded with the low buzz of conversation. The maître d' led them to a candle-lit corner table, then handed them a menu.

"I'll have a dozen of these Malpeque oysters and—hmm. A martini sounds good. How about you?" Wes asked.

Jennie appreciated most fine foods but drew the line at raw oysters. As for drinks, gin was bad enough without adding vermouth. "An Irish coffee for me, and the strawberry cheesecake."

When their orders arrived, each looked at the other's choice askance. "They say opposites attract," Wes smiled. "Let's hope it's an omen." While he squeezed lemon on his oysters, he said, "Shall we compare psyches? I'm an overly ambitious achiever. I thrive on hard work and like to run the whole show myself. How about you?"

Jennie considered the statement, and her answer. Wes hadn't struck her as a particularly hard worker. His easy manner suggested a more laid-back person, although he was obviously an achiever, and she supposed the director held the controls. "I'm a moderately ambitious achiever. I thrive on hard work, too, but a concierge doesn't run the whole show. She just helps it run smoothly."

After testing the first oyster he exclaimed, "These are terrific! Sure you won't try one?"

"Positive, thanks."

"Not venturesome, huh? No interest in new experiences. How's the cheesecake?"

She failed to take the bait. "Marvelous. It's the real thing, not a mix. That's something I appreciate—the real, genuine thing."

"I don't like this," he frowned with mock severity. "We're supposed to be opposites. *I* like the genuine thing, too."

Jennie had acquired the knack of light and amusing conversation and replied, "You wouldn't know the genuine thing if you fell over it. Your whole career is based on make-believe. It's all smoke and light and illusion."

Wes came to attention, surprised to hear the obliging concierge differ with him. "*Au contraire!*" he said. "I suppose I can say *au contraire* in Montreal without sounding pretentious? I insist on authenticity in my films."

"Like substituting Quebec for Northern Europe, you mean, and portraying Blanche Laure as a long-suffering heroine?"

"Ah!" He hesitated a moment, thinking. Even though I must work within the confines of a budget, I insist on authenticity. It wasn't feasible to film in Russia. Canada provided the perfect backdrop for my picture."

Jennie looked unconvinced. "We have something else in common—improvising. It's the concierge's creed."

"You're right about the illusion, though," he conceded. "I did begin by saying I like the genuine thing. I would love to have filmed in Russia."

"You give up too easily." She smiled. "You could have told me how closely you stuck to the novel, or how all the costumes were historically researched."

"We had to cut half the novel, approximately eight hundred pages. As for authentic costumes, we had to work around Blanche's aversion to fur. The Orphan was draped in assorted wolf and bearskins for half the book. We had to use synthetic materials.

"You were going to tell me about Blanche's eccentricity," she said. "Is there a correlation between killing the white tiger and her refusal to wear fur?"

"In a way there is. At an interview back in the States after the event, she took an oath she'd never eat meat or wear fur again. The animal rights people jumped on it and made her a heroine. Now she's stuck with it, much to her chagrin. And mine. A pity she couldn't develop an allergy to jewels. The diamonds in the court scene are genuine."

Jennie exclaimed, "You had to buy diamonds for one scene?"

"No, no. I never buy anything I can get free. Don't look that way! We're talking about film producing. One of the large companies loaned us diamonds. We gave them a plug in the credits."

Jennie nodded. "We can add conniving to your list of characteristics."

Wes was amused at her conversation. It was a welcome change to be with a beautiful young woman who didn't try to butter him up in the hope of getting into films. "It's called good managerial skill," he explained. "How far have we gone into my analysis? I can't offer competent argument. I give up. I'm a conniver and a phony." He waited expectantly for her contradiction, for some attempt to placate him or to flirt.

"Of the worst sort," she agreed. "You try to pass yourself off as genuine."

He took a sip of his drink, while examining Jennie over the rim. He saw the mischievous smile in her eyes, and decided it was time to put her in her place. "Now that we've torn *my* poor character to shreds, shall we examine yours, Jennie? You're an unambitious young lady, content to be a gofer for the hotel."

She refused to take offence. "How can you accuse me of lacking ambition when you don't know where I started from? And I'm not a gofer. I'm in a service-oriented industry that offers great opportunities for advancement."

"But I still say you're underemployed at that job. A woman with your social skills could do better."

"It pays well enough. I don't think just in terms of money. I enjoy working with people and I'm good at it. I meet a lot of interesting people."

His eyes twinkled mischievously. "Like movie stars, you mean?"

"And the mayor. I've had a few words with him. Also authors. I had an interesting talk with Mr. Makepiece, this afternoon. He explained the meaning of his title, *Ring of Fire*. There's an old myth about scorpions and how the natives used to catch them. Apparently, when scorpions are surrounded by a ring of fire, they commit suicide by stinging themselves to death," she explained.

Wes began to wonder just how many of these little chats Jennie and Art Makepiece had had. A celebrated author could prove to be stiff competition. He realized with an unpleasant jolt that he was jealous. "I wouldn't think a scorpion, lurking in some tropical waste, would find himself surrounded by a ring of fire very often," he said, in a disparaging tone.

"In Art's book, it's a symbol of a man surrounded by—well, I haven't read the book yet," she said. "But I imagine the hero's surrounded by danger, and I know there's a suicide in it."

Wes had heard enough about Art Makepiece and reverted to the original topic. "Why did you become a concierge?"

"Why do you make movies?" Jennie asked a little later.

"For the same reasons that you work as a concierge. I enjoy it, and I'm good at it. Shall we call a truce?"

"You're conceding defeat?" she teased.

"It's a truce, not capitulation," he insisted, and quickly changed the subject again. "Where are you from, Jennie?"

"The Eastern Townships, southeast of Montreal. My Dad has a dairy farm there. My brother will take it over, eventually."

"You wanted to see the bright lights?" he asked, trying to picture this petite woman milking a cow.

"I want to see everything," she said comprehensively. "Mom thought I should marry the farmer next door, but I held out and moved to Montreal. It seemed so huge and lonesome at first, until I met people. It's just the first step for me. The first is the hardest, they say."

"They're right." He nodded. "I come from a small town myself. My Dad has a garage. I wasn't much good at technical things. My interests were always more artistic."

Jennie was surprised to hear he was from a small town. "What part of the States are you from, Wes?"

"Sausalito, outside San Francisco." The names sounded exotic to Jennie, conjuring up images of the Pacific Ocean and palm trees.

"It sounds lovely!"

"Have you ever been to California?" he asked.

"Not yet. I've been to Florida, but not the west coast. I plan to see all of North America. I want to work a few years in New York, Chicago, L.A. and perhaps Europe. That's one of the advantages of my job. You're highly mobile."

"That doesn't sound as if you ever intend to marry and settle down." He watched her closely.

Jennie just shrugged. "Maybe, some day. There's a big world out there and I want to see it all. You must have traveled a lot in your work. Have you ever filmed in South America?"

They talked about the places Wes had worked and the places Jennie wished to see. He told her amusing anecdotes about famous people and filmmaking, and she recounted some of her experiences in her work. Wes suggested another drink, but she glanced at her watch and said, "We'd better call it a night."

This too surprised him. "It's early! Don't you believe in the old adage, work hard and play hard?"

"Not on weekdays. Besides I have to drive," she explained.

Wes rose and got her coat. As he put it around her shoulders, he inclined his head and said in a low voice, "I'm looking forward to the weekend."

Jennie felt a tingle of excitement shiver up her spine; whether it emanated from the intimacy of his voice in her ear or the suggestion in the words she wasn't sure. But it seemed a good idea to squelch any growing familiarity.

"Me, too. I'm going skiing," she said, inventing the trip on the spot. Wes could hardly belive it. Another attempt shot down. "Can I drop you at the hotel? It's no trouble, right on my way," she offered.

"When I go out with a lady, I like to see her home. Why don't I drive home with you, and call a cab from there?"

That could be a gentlemanly suggestion or a hint to get into her apartment. In either case, she didn't intend to go along with it. "Let's keep it simple. I'll drop you off at the hotel. It's on my way home."

Wes didn't argue. He went with her to get the car. In the freezing weather, the windshield was frosted, and the motor was sluggish. "I'd better let it warm up before we leave," she suggested.

She huddled into her cozy fur and tried to think of an interesting topic to pass the next few minutes. "You wouldn't have this problem in L.A.," she said.

Wes turned an anticipatory smile on her. She knew as soon as she saw it that he was going to give her a hard time. "I look on a problem as a challenge, even an opportunity," he said, and put one arm around her shoulder. "We'll keep each other warm," he said, in his languid, insinuating way. His arm tightened and drew her against him.

"My fur keeps me warm as toast," she replied, moving away. "I told you a fur wasn't just a fashion accessory here."

"How about sharing the warmth?" His arm pushed the coat aside and went around her waist. The soft smoothness of cashmere was an invitation. He moved his fingers, savoring the texture of the wool, and the sensuous body heat beneath it. His fingers tightened.

Jennie turned to face him and object. His head inclined to her, and she found herself hypnotized by the obsidian glitter of his eyes, which had turned to black in the dim half light. The words died on her lips, as she waited for what would come next. There was a moment of hushed waiting and looking.

It was not an attack, but a leisurely kiss. She had ample opportunity to draw away. Instead she found herself cooperating and enjoying it. The absurd thought occurred to her that at least he couldn't say she was afraid of a new experience. And she soon realized that kissing Wes Adler was an entirely new experience.

Nothing had prepared her for the racing of the blood in her veins and the surge of emotion that swelled when his other hand brushed intimately against the nape of her neck and steadied her head for a deep kiss. It was like diving into deep and dangerous water. Wes was guiding her through uncharted territory. She recognized that he was an expert at this sort of thing. His lips firmed, and his hands began moving in sinuous strokes over her. The one at her neck brushed gently forward and spread along her jaw, leaving a trail of embers where it touched. Then his fingers sought her throat and rested there, clinging warmly to her flesh.

The other hand slid possessively over her back, turning her body to face his, pulling her tightly against him. Her ripe breasts met the firmness of his chest and shaped themselves to it. She felt his hand go lower, measuring her waist, then sliding down to her hips, to pull her yet closer to him. She felt as if something inside her was blossoming, flowering. When his tongue touched her unsteady lips, there was a stunning jolt that stirred the vital core of her being.

A shiver of fear, mingled with desire, quivered through her. She knew she should withdraw but felt incapable of doing it. She felt like a scorpion, surrounded by that riveting ring of fire. It was emotional suicide to let him do this to her. She should... Then his tongue was stroking her lips with tantalizing temptation. What would it be like? Her lips opened almost against her wishes, and the fire moved beyond her lips, licking at her with a disturbing, and engrossing intimacy.

When had his other hand moved to her breast? It rested there now, stroking her with the easy familiarity of possession. Under her dress, she felt her nipples pucker in response to his touch. He felt it, and caught the tip of her breast gently between his fingers, while his tongue continued its assault on her senses.

Wes was a little confused. If a woman enjoyed the game of love, and Jennie certainly didn't seem to mind, why didn't she participate? Her passivity felt like permission, but she didn't add anything to the proceedings. After a moment, he drew back and looked at her questioningly.

"What am I doing wrong?" he asked.

Her dark eyes looked perfectly bewildered. Her breath was labored, and she swallowed before answering. "Whatever you're doing, I'd say you're doing it very well," she said in a small, confused voice.

Not even a farmer's daughter could be this innocent, but he had to hand it to her, she was giving an Oscar winning performance. "Making love is like the tango, Jennie. It takes two."

"Making love!" she exclaimed. "We were just—"

"That's because you weren't cooperating. Of course, it's as cold as hell in here."

A little miffed at his attitude, Jennie said, "Haven't you heard? Hell's hot."

He dampened a sardonic reply. This was no time to start an argument. "Shall we go to your place?" he suggested. "The hotel doesn't seem like a good idea."

Jennie didn't know whether she was more embarrassed or angry. He assumed that because she'd let him kiss her, she was ready for a one-night stand with a man she'd never see after this week. In fairness, however, she admitted that she had probably given him the wrong idea. She didn't answer, but just put the car in gear and drove off.

She took him right to the door of the hotel. Wes didn't suspect anything until she had pulled up under the lighted canopy. With the doorman greeting them, he realized this wasn't the time to discuss it. That, of course, was exactly why she'd done it. Rather a clever trick. The farmer's daughter was no one's fool, but she wasn't dealing with some high school kid.

Didn't she know the *tease* had gone out with felt skirts and hula hoops? Did she really imagine he'd be so foolish as to fall for that ancient trick?

"See you tomorrow, Wes," she said blandly. "Oh, and thanks for inviting me to the play. It was lovely."

He gave her a scathing look. "I enjoyed your performance too, Jennie. I'm looking forward to act two."

The doorman assisted him out of the car and he left, without looking back.

He went straight to his room to take a shower. He had been interested in Jennie from the beginning. By being— or pretending to be—unimpressed by his job, she had accelerated his attraction. He wasn't used to courting a woman. His more usual problem was trying to escape their advances. Of course, she'd been interested all along or she wouldn't have met him tonight and led him on.

His pride was stung, and when Wescott Adler was offended he didn't turn tail and run. He fought back. The question was, how to win a battle with a flirt? It was a woman's game. A flirting man would look ridiculous. He would have to put her in her place.

Let her think he was besotted, then walk off without a backward glance? At the premiere, with the press hounding him, and when she read the reviews of *Orphan* later,

Jennie would realize what a catch he was, if she didn't know it already. Unfortunately, they'd be leaving the day after the premiere. That didn't leave him much time. Besides, she might really fall in love with him, and if she did that would be cruel. No, a more fitting punishment would be to ignore her and shower Blanche with attention. As he toweled himself and shrugged into the terry housecoat, he looked dangerously determined.

Jennie drove home without incident and without traffic mishaps. She had been pleasantly surprised with the first part of the evening. Wes Adler was really very nice for such an important man. She was fully aware of his eminence; moreover, she admired him for not flaunting it. But when she thought of the debacle in the parking lot, she felt hot with shame. What must he think of her? She had acted like those women her mother called "no better than they should be." He had been presumptuous in thinking she was going to invite him to stay overnight.

She decided it was culture shock, that's all. In Hollywood, that sort of thing was common. She read enough magazines to know that. Life was different in a French Catholic farming community, and Jennie hadn't changed that much since leaving home. She wished she'd never have to see Wes Adler again, but since she did she'd just treat him like any other customer. She'd be polite and pleasant, and she wouldn't be alone with him if she could help it.

Once this was decided, she went to bed, determined to put him out of her mind. Then she spent the next half hour wondering how to behave with Wes tomorrow. He'd be seeing her even if they weren't going to be alone, and she was interested enough that she wanted to leave a good impression.

Chapter Six

In the morning, Jennie was tempted to wear her hair unbraided, the way Wes liked it. It took a conscious effort to overcome the urge, but she succeeded. For work, it looked better in its usual French braid. More professional, and professional was the way she intended to behave toward Wes Adler. She was sorting her mail and looking over her messages when she heard a tap at her door. Wes! Her heart quickened and she felt a splotch of warmth grow on her cheeks. "Come in," she called.

It was only R.K. Benson, resplendent that day in a butter yellow turtleneck and plaid trousers. "Morning, J.M.," he said, throwing himself on to a chair.

"Can I do something for you?" she asked briskly, to let him know she was busy.

"I need some advice, and since you're the resident expert, I came to you. We need to plan an activity for Blanche today, have you got any ideas? Something to keep her in the limelight."

"There's a snow fair at McGill. She might put in an appearance there," Jennie suggested. "It'll be covered by the media, TV and the papers."

R.K. considered it. "Let's choose an event that wouldn't lure groups of pretty young coeds, know what I mean? Something indoors, preferably. The wind dries her skin."

"The Museum of Fine Arts is opening a new exhibit today. Monet and Seurat."

"Great! Blanche loves culture. I'll tell her. What time is the opening?"

Jennie checked her files. "Two-thirty. Admission to the opening is by invitation only. I'm sure they'd be delighted to have Blanche there."

R.K. went to her phone, and after he had pushed the buttons, secured it between his chin and shoulder to speak. He didn't have to, since he wasn't writing with his other hand. Jennie decided it was just one more little affectation from an inhabitant of tinsel town.

"Blanche, R.K. here. I've got something you might like. I'll run it by you. It's the opening of some art exhibit. You always enjoy cultural things. And it'll give you something to talk about tonight with that Minister of Culture at the ball." Blanche's throaty voice could be heard clearly from the receiver, then R.K. spoke again. "The artists? Monet and—I'll let the concierge tell you," he said, handing the phone to Jennie. "She wants to know whose works are being shown."

Jennie took the phone and explained. "The exhibition is highlighting the French impressionists, Ms. Laure. Monet and Seurat, and I think a few Renoirs."

"I believe I met Monet once," Blanche said pensively.

Jennie bit her lips to keep from smiling. "It couldn't have been Claude. He's been dead for sixty years. It must have been some other Monet, Ms. Laure," she suggested discreetly.

"Silly me! I meant Manet, of course." Jennie refrained form telling her Manet had been dead even longer. She thought Ms. Laure wouldn't take kindly to corrections. "In any case, I adore the expressionists. Have R.K. notify the press I'll be there. Thank you, dear."

"You're welcome." Jennie winced at Blanche's obvious patronization as she hung up. "You'd better warn Ms. Laure Monet is an impressionist, not an expressionist. You wouldn't want her making a gaffe like that in public."

"Blanche is like the Queen of Hearts. Words mean what she says they mean."

"Not to the Minister of Culture, they don't. I think you should warn her." She also explained about Manet and Monet.

"Will do. Thanks for the tip, J.M. Is there any action on that suite next to hers? You mentioned it would be vacated today. She's missing Wes. The sly rascal slipped the leash last night. She didn't like that," he said, and smiled in a knowing way. "Of course, no one has told her who he was with. I suggest you keep it under your curls, too. Make that—braid."

Jennie didn't like to gossip, but she'd been wondering how deeply Wes and Blanche were involved, and said, "I thought she was married?"

"Blanche marries, from time to time. She last married a decade ago. That's kaput. If she ever decided to do the middle aisle two-step again, she'll get a divorce, I suppose. This way, it's all informal, therefore, she doesn't get stuck with heavy-duty alimony."

"Are she and Wes thinking of getting married?" she asked, feigning a casual tone.

"Yours truly would be the last to know," he said, with a shrug, "but Wes instructed me not to tell her he was out with you last night."

It hurt like a knife in the chest. She didn't mean a thing to Wes Adler. She was just a little diversion, someone he amused himself with. "I'll make that room switch right away." She didn't even want to talk to Wes on the phone. "Maybe you could inform him? I'm a little busy."

"I'll arrange it with Blanche," he said.

It sounded as if he wanted to take the credit for arranging Wes's move but Jennie couldn't have cared less. "You can get the keys at the desk," she said, and picked up a letter to give R.K. a hint to leave.

"Rightie-ho, I'll handle it. Wes is tied up today with some exploratory work on his new film project. He and a few of his aides are taking a lunch meeting downtown."

"Fine, see you later."

R.K. left, and Jennie continued with her work. She tried to push Wes to the back of her mind, but he kept resurfacing. Blanche and Wes, in adjoining rooms. He'd ordered another four dozen red roses, and tonight he'd be accompanying her to the minister's dinner and ball. He didn't mind letting her know he was going out with Blanche, but he didn't want Blanche to know he was seeing another woman. He was just a man on the make. Forget him.

Blanche took her usual walk with Ruby that morning. Bereft of Wes, she had lunch with R.K. and others in her entourage. Stuffing herself with meat, which she called vegetables. All of them were as phony as three dollar bills. Jennie didn't even know why she bothered peeking out to see what Blanche was wearing when she took off for the art opening. Except that there was just something irresistible about seeing in the flesh the people you usually only saw on the screen.

One expected them to be different from ordinary people. If Blanche Laure acted like the girl next door, she wouldn't be as intriguing or as exciting. She certainly didn't look like any girl Jennie had ever lived next door to. She swaggered out of the hotel in a snow white coat with a flaring back. With it she wore long black gloves and high black leather boots. Or maybe they were vinyl, since she was such a great animal rights activist.

Jennie had to arrange an appointment with an orthodontist for a young guest who had gotten a paper clip stuck in his braces. There was also a large wedding anniversary party to organize. A fortieth anniversary. The smaller reception room had to be decorated and a violinist met with her to receive instructions. The friend of the couple celebrating the anniversary was supposed to meet him, but never showed. "Improvise," Jennie muttered to herself, and suggested the traditional tunes.

Later, Mr. Simon reported that the entire set of towels from Room 316 was missing.

"Shall I write and mention the oversight that may have occurred in packing?" Jennie suggested, using the standard euphemism for theft.

"It's the Willards. Better not. They're very high class. The towels will probably be used at their pool. Good advertising. Amazing though, that people like that would snitch the linen. I'm beginning to think we should sell them."

"We could have the gift shop stock them," Jennie suggested. "Some hotels do."

"The Ritz doesn't," he replied. That was always the criterion used.

At four-thirty, Blanche returned from the museum. Jennie assumed the visit had gone well because she was smiling. Her smile would no doubt broaden once she found Wes had been transferred to the room beside her.

A little later, Jennie went to the small reception room to check on the flowers and table arrangement. When she returned to her office, Wes was just entering the hotel. Jennie felt a rush of excitement, but tried desperately not to show it.

He gave her a lukewarm grin and said, "Is Blanche in her room?"

"Yes, she just returned a moment ago." Jennie was about to tell him of the room transfer, but he had already turned to leave.

Wes noticed that little beam of anticipation. Was Jennie having second thoughts about her abrupt treatment of him already? He turned. "Good, I'm very eager to see her. Thanks, Ms. Longman." The formality came very naturally, as he had been mentally rehearsing it. He saw the look of surprise, tinged with irritation she directed at him, and decided to give the needle another jab. "Would you send a bottle of champagne and two glasses up to her room, please? And hold any calls till further notice. We won't want to be disturbed."

"Certainly, Mr. Adler. Dom Pérignon?"

"Please. Nothing but the best for Blanche."

"And a filet mignon for the dog?" Jennie asked. Her tone was polite, but there was anger in her eyes. They looked like green fire today. "Or is this a private celebration?"

"Hold the steak. This is private," he said, then strolled away.

Jennie didn't bother to tell him about the room transfer after that meaningful speech. Let Blanche do it, since that was where he was headed. She ordered the champagne and returned to her desk. "Ms. Longman," was it? He was probably afraid Blanche would hear about it if he called her Jennie in the hotel. Those familiarities were reserved for when he was away from Blanche, out on the prowl.

She was furious with herself for having broken her own rule. She never should have gone out with Wes Adler. *Mr.* Adler. It was pretty clear what he was after. Since she wasn't interested in an affair, he was quick to reestablish more professional relations. The champagne and roses were reserved for the obliging Blanche. She shouldn't have made that crack about the dog, though, putting it on the same level as Blanche. Next time she spoke to Wes, she'd be just as polite and formal as he was.

Jennie had her chance to practice the new politeness. Five minutes later, Wes came storming into her office without even knocking. His gray eyes blazed with fury, and his face was livid with rage.

"What kind of a hotel is this?" he demanded. Without waiting for an answer, he pounced forward and pounded one closed fist on her desk. "I didn't give an order to have my room changed!"

Jennie, who felt vulnerable while sitting down, jumped to her feet to defend herself. "We discussed it the day you arrived. You said it would be ideal."

"It isn't ideal now." Since he needed some excuse for this about-face, he added, "All my work and papers are in a mess. It'll take hours to sort them out. I want to know who's responsible for this."

R.K. Benson had urged the move on her, but Jennie didn't want to get him in trouble. He had to work with Adler in the future. She only had to put up with him for a few more days. Her chin tilted upwards and she said, "I am. I gave the order. Ms. Laure was eager for the change,'' she added, since Blanche could obviously handle him.

Calling her name was like waving a red flag in front of Wes. He'd have Blanche in his room every two minutes, trailing her dog after her. She was troublesome enough with two floors between them.

"Ms. Laure is not in charge of my life. When I want to move, *I'll* give the order. Till that time, I'd thank you to keep out of my room."

"I wasn't in it!" she objected.

"You let somebody make a hell of a mess. I'm returning to my old room, immediately. I won't expect to be charged for that arbitrary move made behind my back."

"I'll send someone up—"

"No! I don't want anyone touching my papers."

"I'm sorry your papers were disturbed, Mr. Adler, but since you're already in the rooms you wanted in the first place, why bother to move again?"

Her suggestion was completely logical. Wes remembered implying he wanted the room beside Blanche's. It had seemed safe, since it was occupied at the time. With no sensible answer to save face, he had to resort to another outburst.

"Is this a new policy, that the guests in your hotel have to live with the mistakes of management? I did *not* ask to be transferred. I do *not* want the new rooms you've allotted me. They're cramped and noisy, on top of everything else."

"They're identical to the rooms you have now. And much more convenient to Ms. Laure." Instead of consoling Wes, this reminder had the effect of raising his temperature to an even higher degree. He looked as if he would explode, and to forestall it Jennie raced on. "If you

```
**********************************************************
*  You may have already won a lifetime of **cash payments** *
*  **totaling up to $1,000,000.00!**  Play our Sweepstakes  *
*  Game--**Here's how it works...**                          *
**********************************************************
```

Each of the first three tickets has a unique Sweepstakes number
If your Sweepstakes numbers match any of the winning numbers
selected by our computer, you could win the amount shown under
the gold rub-off on that ticket.

Using an eraser, rub off the gold boxes on tickets #1-3 to
reveal how much each ticket could be worth if it is a winning
ticket. You must return the <u>entire</u> card to be eligible. (See
official rules in the back of this book for details.)

At the same time you play your tickets for big cash prizes,
Silhouette also invites you to participate in a special trial o
our Reader Service by accepting one or more FREE book(s) from
Silhouette Romance.™ To request your free book(s), just rub off
the gold box on ticket #4 to reveal how many free book(s) you
will receive.

When you receive your free book(s), we hope you'll enjoy them
and want to see more. So unless we hear from you, every month
we'll send you 6 additional Silhouette Romance™novels. Each
book is yours to keep for only $2.25* each. There are <u>no</u>
additional charges for shipping and handling and of course, you
may cancel Reader Service privileges at any time by marking
"cancel" on your shipping statement or returning an unopened
shipment of books to us at our expense. Either way your
shipments will stop. You'll receive no more books; you'll have
no further obligation.

PLUS-you get a FREE MYSTERY GIFT!

If you return your game card with <u>**all four gold boxes**</u> rubbed
off, you will also receive a FREE Mystery Gift. It's your
<u>**immediate reward**</u> for sampling your free book(s), <u>**and**</u> it's yours
to keep no matter what you decide.

P.S.

Remember, the first set of one or more book(s) is FREE. So rub
off the gold box on ticket #4 and return the entire sheet of
tickets today!

*Terms and prices subject to change without notice.
 Sales taxes applicable in New York and Iowa.

"GIVE YOUR HEART TO SILHOUETTE" SWEEPSTAKES

DETACH HERE AND RETURN ENTIRE SHEET OF TICKETS NOW!

#1 **$1,000,000.00**

Rub off to reveal potential value if this is a winning ticket: ►

UNIQUE SWEEPSTAKES NUMBER: 6A 384477

#2 **$1,000,000.00**

Rub off to reveal potential value if this is a winning ticket: ►

UNIQUE SWEEPSTAKES NUMBER: 7A 386462

#3 **$1,000,000.00**

Rub off to reveal potential value if this is a winning ticket: ►

UNIQUE SWEEPSTAKES NUMBER: 8A 384128

#4 **ONE OR MORE FREE BOOKS**

HOW MANY FREE BOOKS?
Rub off to reveal number of free books you will receive ►

1672765559

Yes! Enter my sweepstakes numbers in the Sweepstakes and let me know if I've won a cash prize. If gold box on ticket **#4** is rubbed off, I will also receive one or more Silhouette Romance novels as a FREE tryout of the Reader Service, along with a FREE Mystery Gift as explained on the opposite page. 215 CIS HAX8

NAME

ADDRESS APT.

CITY STATE ZIP CODE

Offer not valid to current Silhouette Romance subscribers. All orders subject to approval. PRINTED IN U.S.A.

DON'T FORGET...

...Return this card today with ticket #4 rubbed off, and receive 4 free books and a free mystery gift.

...You will receive books well before they're available in stores.

...No obligation to buy. You can cancel at any time by writing "cancel" on your statement or returning an unopened shipment to us at our cost.

BUSINESS REPLY CARD

First Class   Permit No. 717   Buffalo, NY

Postage will be paid by addressee

Silhouette Reader Service ™

MILLION DOLLAR SWEEPSTAKES

901 Fuhrmann Blvd.
P.O. Box 1867
Buffalo, N.Y. 14240-9952

NO POSTAGE
NECESSARY
IF MAILED
IN THE
UNITED STATES

want to go back to your old room, please go ahead. You still have the keys.''

''I'm surprised you haven't got someone else in my bed, by now!''

''I'm afraid you'll have to make that arrangement yourself, Mr. Adler. I'm sure you won't have any trouble.'' The impetuous speech was made before Jennie had a chance to censor it. She had broken the prime rule of the concierge. She had lost her temper, and she had been rude to a very important guest. To make matters worse, she had no intention of apologizing. Mr. Adler had told her himself he wanted those rooms as soon as they were available. She had only done her duty.

She gave a fearful glance at Wes. Her heart pounded in her chest and her breaths came in short, shallow gasps. He'd give her hell, then he'd march to Simon's office and have her fired. She felt it in her bones. A whole miserable future flashed before her eyes, while she stood staring at his cold, implacable face, with those gray eyes blazing at her.

To her astonishment, his muscles relaxed slightly, and a cynical smile curved his lips. ''So you *do* have a temper,'' he said. ''I was beginning to think Montreal's ice had frozen you.''

Before Jennie could reply, there was a tap at the door and R.K. Benson came in. ''Do I sense a little hostility in the air?'' he asked, glancing uncertainly from one to the other. ''Sorry about the snafu, Wes. My fault. I take complete blame. When Blanche found out those rooms were empty, she hounded me to death and I urged J.M. to make the switcheroo.''

Jennie was grateful, and a little surprised, that R.K. spoke up. To show her appreciation, she said, ''I should have checked with Mr. Adler first to see that he hadn't changed his mind. It won't happen again."

The phone pealed, and she was relieved for the diversion. The atmosphere was so tense you could feel it. It was a French-speaking customer on the phone, and she slipped easily into the language. *"Ah, Monsieur Dupré. Au sujet du dîner pour vos amis ... vous aurez la même petite salle à manger que jadis."*

Wes listened. It was strange how a foreign language changed the whole image of a person. He had often used the trick himself in his films. German, with its harsh gutturals, lent a touch of danger. French was definitely romantic. The mouth moved in a seductive way, as if Jennie was preparing her lips for a kiss. Even the timbre of her voice sounded different. More alluring. When she gave a low, conspiratorial laugh, he found himself wondering who Monsieur Dupré might be. She sounded very friendly. Was he a customer or a friend? It seemed even less possible that she was as innocent as she pretended.

She soon hung up and turned back to them in her English mood.

"Very impressive, J.M.," Benson said. "French lends a real touch of class to a lady, don't you agree, Wes?" Wes just looked at him without answering.

"Most business people in Quebec are bilingual," Jennie said dismissingly.

"This is one terrific lady," R.K. added. "She kept Blanche from making a fool of herself at the opening today, as well. You know Blanche and art. She recognizes two names: Leonardo and Picasso."

Wes looked interested, and Benson mentioned the impressionist show that Blanche had mistaken for expressionist, and the confusion of artists' names.

Jennie felt pink with embarrassment at the praise and said rather abruptly, "My neighbor's a teacher at the Beaux Arts. She talks about art a lot. I don't really know that much about it."

"What you do know was useful," Benson smiled. "Blanche is a quick study. I'll say that for her. She managed to work the things you told her into the conversation."

Benson showed no signs of leaving. Wes said, "Would you mind going to my room to see that no one touches my research papers, R.K.? That's my new room," he added, giving Jennie a little smile.

She knew something had happened to soften his anger. Perhaps it was R.K.'s taking the blame. That was it. He'd apologize and leave.

R.K. said, "Consider it done, chief. Oh, and incidentally, the bubbly has arrived. Blanche is waiting." Then he left.

Wes leaned against the front of Jennie's desk and said, "Why didn't you tell me I was out of line?"

"I should have checked with you first," she replied. "Although, I understood you wanted the transfer as soon as possible."

His dark eyes seemed to hold a question as he studied her. Wes liked people who owned up to their mistakes. It was one of the reasons he tolerated R.K. That, and Blanche's high opinion of him. But to take responsibility for someone else's errors went beyond the call of duty. There was a lot more to Jennie Longman than just a pretty face. She was that rare species, a person of integrity and as innocent as she seemed. And he had made a flaming jackass of himself in front of her.

He let the subject drop. "Where did you learn to speak French so fluently?" he asked.

"At home. This is Quebec. French is the official language."

"Maybe I should be asking where you learned English?"

"We spoke English at home. My mom's French-Canadian. At the convent school, we spoke only French. The nuns insisted on it. Since the French are surrounded by English provinces, they're afraid of losing their native tongue."

She hadn't mentioned going to a convent school before. In her dark suit with the prim white blouse, it was easy to imagine Jennie in a school uniform. That kind of training left an indelible stamp. Benson was right. This was one terrific lady.

"I'm shooting my next film in France," he said pensively.

She glanced at her watch. "How interesting," she said, but she didn't ask any questions.

"None of my crew actually knows the language."

"I expect you'll have to hire a few translators."

"That's one answer." From the way he said it, it didn't sound like the answer he wanted to hear.

"Your champagne will be getting warm," she said, to remind him.

"This time I won't blame you. What would I do without you? I could really use a personal secretary, to keep me on track."

"You already have one."

"Not a personal one. Ms. Cousens just handles company business."

Jennie gave him a slightly mocking look. "I wondered why she didn't order Ms. Laure's flowers for you."

"She can do it next time, if you don't care for the job."

"I don't mind in the least, Mr. Adler. I'm always happy to look after the hotel's guests. It's my job. Will there be anything else?"

"I'll let you know. See you later. And Jennie, I'm sorry about—my temper tantrum."

His mood was completely softened now. She was surprised at that apology, and the "Jennie." In spite of herself, she felt her anger dissolve. "We expect it from you movie people." She smiled.

"We're not all freaks and phonies, you know."

"Of course not," she murmured, with complete insincerity.

Wes left, unhappy with himself. He had planned to let Jennie think he and Blanche were a major item. She had taken it at face value and didn't seem to mind a bit. Now where did he go from here? She hadn't turned a hair at that hint of working for him. She wasn't the least bit interested.

Jennie shuffled her papers into neat piles and examined her desk. The last moments replayed themselves in her mind. Had Wes—Mr. Adler—been hinting that he might offer her a job? Personally, she couldn't think of anything more tiresome than being a Hollywood yes-man. She didn't have to work for him to go to France. With her second language, she could get a good job in one of the finer hotels with no trouble.

The Hollywood contingent would be out at the minister's dinner and ball this evening, and she was happy to leave work at the usual time. It felt good to get away from them, with all their petty problems. Yet, as she drove home, she admitted that she wouldn't have minded going to that dinner and ball. These shifting feelings about the people in film were something new in her life. You could hate them one minute and love them the next, but it was hard to be indifferent.

Chapter Seven

R.K. Benson came into Jennie's office early the next morning. His yellow sweater had given way to peach, with a large black muffler wrapped around his neck. He was rubbing his hand.

"Did you hurt yourself?" Jennie asked.

"I've been signing Blanche's name on photographs. Her fan club is meeting here today."

"And *you* sign the pictures?" Jennie asked, laughing.

"A liaison's lot is not a happy one. Especially when Blanche is in a huff," he said. "Huff? Did I say huff? Blanche is throwing a full-blown temper tantrum. To say nothing of the statuette she threw at me."

Jennie gave a howl of anguish. "Not the Bustelli. Don't tell me she threw the Bustelli nymph. It's an antique."

R.K. regarded her warily. "So high," he said, measuring about eight inches. "Blue and white dress."

"It was the Bustelli," Jennie said weakly.

"Now a busted Bustelli, an ex-Bustelli."

"We shouldn't have left it in her room. I should have known after she broke the Sèvres vase. What will I tell Simon?"

R.K. tried to console her. "Wes will pay. He always does. It was good of you to share the flack yesterday, J.M. I appreciate it."

"Flack-catching is part of my job. What is behind her poor temper today?" Jennie asked, trying to take her mind off the Bustelli nymph.

"That minister's ball last night was a bust. Strictly stuffed shirts."

"Everyone was there. It was the best party in town," Jennie objected.

"You should have warned us they were importing competition from Paris. Blanche prefers to be the only star in the galaxy. They had two other mega film stars, plus one world-renowned chanteuse. And since Blanche doesn't *parlez français*, she was way out in the cold."

"The minister and his group speak English," Jennie said.

"I don't mean she was ignored. The French actors spoke some English, too. She just wasn't the center of the universe. There were major gales upstairs when she got home. Of course, Wes's refusal to move in next door didn't help."

Jennie bit her tongue. She would *not* ask why he hadn't taken the room. R.K. read her expression and added, "It's the mutt. Ruby is a restless sleeper. So's Wes. He wouldn't get a wink. Or, at least, that's what he told Blanche."

Jennie didn't think the light barking of a tiny chihuahua could be heard through the thick walls of the hotel. "Is there something you want me to do, R.K.?" she asked.

"Oh, no. I'll handle her. I want your advice on a different matter." He patted his frizzed hair. "I'm going to have my hair straightened. When I saw a banker at last night's affair with a frizz I knew it was time for a change. What do you think—long and straight or cut short? Tell me frankly. Is my face too thin for a brush cut?"

This petty decision was obviously important to R.K., and Jennie thought about it a moment. "I don't think a brush would suit you, but I wouldn't leave it too long. I'm conservative, R.K. I'd get a business cut, something like—like Mr. Adler's," she finished in confusion. "That's just my opinion."

"I think you're right. I'm getting a little old to play the juvenile role. I'll go for it. And maybe a dark suit . . . The thing is, Wes is dangling a good job in front of me if I help him with a little something that I'm not at liberty to disclose. He's hammering out the final details with some investors now."

"What kind of job?" she asked. But for Jennie the more interesting question was "what are you helping Wes with?"

"Assistant to the director. I'd really learn the technical ropes at that guy's elbow. I know the general business inside out. I've been in it for eons. I'm really quite artistic, you know. This is my chance. Wes nearly bowled me over when he broached it last night after dinner. He likes my integrity," he added, frowning.

"The assistant director's job, you would be working on the film he's going to do in France?" she asked.

"That hasn't been announced yet. How did you know about it? Did Wes tell you?" he asked in surprise.

"He didn't say it was a secret. I won't mention it to anyone else."

R.K. gave her a conspiratorial wink. "Don't, or you'll have half of Montreal angling for the job you're after."

"What do you mean? I'm not after a job with him."

R.K. looked at her, disbelieving. "But I thought—I mean with your French and everything. I was sure it was you he meant."

"No, there's some mistake," Jennie insisted. "He dropped a hint, but—"

"But you'd take it if he offered!" R.K. said.

"No, I'm not at all interested. I told Wes—Mr. Adler—so."

R.K. gave a broad wink. "Gotcha. You learn quick. Never accept the first offer. Hang tough and you can probably double it. When Wes wants something, he doesn't care what he has to pay or do to get it. I'm really looking forward to working with you, J.M."

"But I'm not—"

"Mum's the word." He gave a knowing little laugh and left.

The meeting left Jennie dissatisfied and curious. Dissatisfied that Wes, and apparently everyone else, thought she'd jump at the chance of working with him. She was also curious as to what Wes needed R.K.'s help for. The question kept recurring as she worked. So did a memory of the Bustelli nymph. When she told Mr. Simon, he was too overwrought to do more than moan in grief.

Things at the Mont Royal proceeded smoothly for most of the day. Late in the afternoon, Mr. Simon brought the lovely statuette from the penthouse suite in to show Jennie.

"It's only the arms that are broken," he said, studying it. "But a patched figurine isn't worth much. Call the insurance people, will you, and check our coverage? The rates we pay, they damned well should cover it."

"I thought it was safe, since it was on a high shelf and the dog couldn't get at it."

"Thinking isn't what got us into this mess," Mr. Simon said through clenched teeth. Jennie noticed that his enthusiasm for Hollywood had faded even faster than hers. He was counting the days till they all left.

"Ms. Laure is entertaining her fan club with coffee and doughnuts in the small reception room at four," he said.

"What are the Olympia crew doing tonight?"

"Wes arranged a night on the town with some French actors. The celebrities Blanche met last night—thank God. I wonder where they're staying. Probably the Ritz. I really should warn the manager."

The next half hour was lively, with Ms. Laure's fan club arriving in bunches. They were mostly high school and university students, with a handful of aging adults who had followed Blanche's career over the years. Blanche was in a good mood, as she was the undivided center of attention. She played the grande dame, handing out the photographs which R.K. had forged in her name.

As everything was progressing smoothly, Jennie left work at her regular time. She was going to see the exhibit of impressionist paintings at the art gallery with her artist friend and neighbor that evening. They were going to have dinner on the way, to save time.

Her friend, Beckie Hamilton, had suggested it. Beckie was five or six years older than Jennie. She played the role of artiste to the hilt, with her long black hair hanging like a curtain down her back. Her clothes were bohemian. Although she wasn't really pretty, she looked dramatic.

In the dead of winter, slacks were the preferred outfit for a casual evening. They both wore slacks and high boots and their fur coats, with mufflers wrapped around their throats. It was Beckie's turn to drive. Once inside the building, they checked their coats and made a leisurely tour of the exhibit. It was easy to forget the snow and cold as they gazed at the sun-drenched pictures of flowers and meadows. Jennie enjoyed having an expert with her, explaining the nuances of style.

"It's all done by colored spots," Beckie explained. "The subject of the impressionists is really the play of sunlight on an object. To give the dappled effect, they use the component colors. Blue and yellow to make green, you see. Stand back, and they merge to give a wonderfully vivid effect."

Jennie moved back a few paces without looking behind her and bumped into someone. "I'm sorry!" she exclaimed, then looked around.

"I'm not," a lazy, deep voice answered.

It was Wes Adler standing behind her. He looked down and smiled, and she felt a strong churning inside. Wes looked dangerously handsome, with that familiar shock of black hair dangling over his forehead. Even in a rough gray sweater and jeans, he looked fantastic.

"Hi, Jennie. I was wondering if I might find you here. I stopped at your office around six, but you'd left. When you didn't answer your apartment phone..."

Jennie was nonplussed at his speech. He had gone to all that trouble to find her? She recovered her wits and introduced him to Beckie. "Ms. Hamilton is an art instructor," Jennie added.

"I'm pleased to meet you, Beckie. This is the friend you mentioned," he said to Jennie. "Now I know how you know so much about art."

"I don't know much, but Beckie was just explaining the technique of the impressionists."

Wes gave Beckie a charming smile. "May I join the tour?" he asked. Beckie showed no signs of reluctance. "I don't want to give you ladies the idea I'm a panhandler, begging for a free lesson. I'll buy drinks later.''

He put one hand on Beckie's arm, the other on Jennie's and they continued the tour, with Beckie waxing eloquent. She liked an audience, especially a handsome one such as this.

She soon discovered who Wes was, and began peppering him with questions about Blanche and the movie world. Jennie wished her friend wouldn't gush quite so much, but she supposed it was the normal first reaction to a brush with someone from Hollywood.

''It must be thrilling!'' she exclaimed. ''You lucky dog, Jennie.''

''I don't believe Jennie shares your enthusiasm,'' Wes said, with a conspiratorial smile. ''We're causing her a few headaches at the Mont Royal.''

Beckie stared at her friend, bewildered. Her eyes held a hundred questions, but they had moved on to the next painting and Beckie was soon distracted by another art lecture. They stayed at the exhibit for an hour.

''I'm bringing my class over tomorrow,'' Beckie said. ''And I imagine you've seen enough pigment. Shall we have that drink now, folks?''

''That's not necessary,'' Jennie said swiftly. ''I'm sure you were happy to give us the lecture free, Beckie.''

''We were going to have a drink, anyway,'' Beckie said.

''We were going home for coffee,'' Jennie reminded her.

''Right. Well, why don't you join us for coffee at Jennie's place, Wes? I'm dying to hear about Blanche Laure's little dog.''

Wes looked at Jennie. He saw her annoyance and knew she wanted to object. He also knew she was too polite to rob her friend of the pleasure his presence seemed to be giving her.

"All right. We'll have a quick coffee," she agreed, and they left.

"Are you driving, Wes?" Beckie asked.

"I took a cab."

"Then you'll come with me." She smiled.

Jennie hopped into the back seat before any discussion of the seating arrangements arose. Beckie was so excited that she took care of the talking. Jennie just sat there, alone in the dark, wondering how she could let Beckie know she was to stay until after Wes left her apartment. She had no intention of being alone with him. And why wasn't he out with Blanche and the French actors, anyway? Did they have a completely open relationship? Was tonight Blanche's night for a change of companion?

They went up to her apartment and Jennie went to the kitchen immediately to make the coffee, leaving Beckie with Wes in the living room. Beckie was talking his ear off. On top of everything else, Jennie was peeved that Wes and Beckie got on so well together. She heard them laughing like old friends. She brought in the coffee tray and began to pour.

"Wes was just telling me he has a Monet in his home in Bel Air," Beckie said. Her eyes were as big as saucers. "One of the famous water lily series."

He saw Jennie's eyes widen in surprise, just before she assumed an expression of total indifference. He decided to tease her a little. "And a rather handsome little Renoir of a girl holding a bird on the end of of her finger," he added.

"You're a serious collector, then!" Beckie exclaimed. "What else do you have?"

"One of Picasso's fractured women, with an eye in one corner and a mouth in the other, looking as if she'd caught her head in a blender. It's the only one I bought without truly liking it."

"But an artist isn't painting objective reality, Wes. He's painting his interpretation of the model," Beckie explained.

"Yes, of course," he agreed. "But you can't help wondering just how Picasso viewed women, that he painted them so ugly." He saw from the corner of his eye that Jennie was making a great show of indifference, and added mischievously, "I much prefer my Renoir and Modigliani."

"You have a Modigliani, too?" Beckie exclaimed.

Jennie sipped her coffee and tried to look unimpressed. Wes had never mentioned his own life-style, where he lived, that sort of thing. He probably had one of those mansions you saw in books. Beckie began asking questions.

"I bet you have a swimming pool," she said eagerly.

"It gets very warm in L.A. Not like Canada. You ladies have your furs to keep warm—we have our pools to keep cool."

"Do you drive a Rolls?" Beckie asked eagerly. Jennie turned aside and plumped up a cushion.

"A Rolls is pretentious," he replied, glinting a glance at Jennie who refused to look at him. In revenge, he added, "I drive a Bentley for formal occasions. I really prefer my little Mercedes."

Jennie just sat, feigning indifference. Beckie was being impossible, but why was Wes going along with this game of show and tell? He sounded worse than R.K. Benson. While they talked, she made a mental tour of her own apartment. The artworks were mostly framed posters, with one original oil painting she'd bought from one of Beckie's students. In the garage there was one used car. She didn't have a pool or any of those other luxuries.

The conversation had reverted to art again. "What technique do you use, Beckie?" Wes was asking.

"Why don't you come to my place and I'll show you?"

Wes looked at Jennie. "Shall we?" he asked.

"You run along, Wes. I've seen Beckie's lovely paintings many times. I'll just take these dishes to the kitchen while you two go." She started collecting the cups.

They left, and that angered Jennie, too. If he'd gone to the gallery looking for her, why was he running off to Beckie's place? She'd put the cups in the sink, to give them the hint there wasn't going to be any more coffee. It was ten o'clock, and she was strongly tempted to go to bed, but they'd left their coats behind. Her hand went unconsciously to Wes's, stroking it. When she noticed what she was doing, she pulled her hand away as if the coat were aflame.

They returned in about ten minutes. "I've brought your friend back," Beckie said, revealing a guilty smile. "Sorry if I monopolized him. I'll just get my coat and run. It was lovely meeting you, Wes. Be sure to tell Blanche Laure how much I like her work."

"I certainly will," he said.

Wes took Beckie's coat and handed it to her at the door to keep his hands busy. That way, Jennie couldn't give him his coat. His triumphant little grin told her he had done it on purpose.

"See you tomorrow, Jennie," Beckie waved.

"Thanks for the guided tour, Beckie."

Beckie Hamilton left, and Jennie handed Wes his coat. "Aren't you even going to call me a cab?" he asked. "It's mighty cold to be standing on a street corner, waiting."

"Sorry. I forgot," she said, and went to make the call. Wes followed her, and when she reached for the phone he took it from her and set it down.

"It's only ten o'clock," he said. "We haven't had a minute to talk."

She tossed her head unconcernedly. "I heard every word you said. You don't have to repeat that you have a pool and a luxurious car and priceless art, et cetera."

Wes cocked his head on one side and grinned. "I was terrible, wasn't I?"

"Yes and I can't imagine why, unless you were trying to impress Beckie. Of course, she's very pretty," Jennie added, studying him.

That expression on his face didn't look as if he cared a hoot about Beckie. "Can't you?" he asked, taking her hand to lead her to the sofa. She was curious enough to hear him out. "I was trying to seduce you," he said blandly.

Jennie just looked, unable to believe he'd come right out and said it. "Don't faint!" he continued. "There's more than one kind of seduction. You know I want you to come and work for me. I was just giving you an idea of the working conditions. It's very nice in California."

"I thought it was my French you were interested in, since your next project will be filmed in France."

Wes nodded. "That was an added attraction. But it's really your organizational skills and the way you handle people that interests me." His dark eyes studied her, flickering from the glow of her hair, over her bewitching green eyes, down to her little pointed chin. She looked like an angry kitten, and he felt a nearly overpowering urge to kiss her.

Watching him, Jennie had an idea what was on his mind. Her heart thumped erratically, and her throat suddenly felt bone dry. It wasn't a job he was offering; he wanted a mistress. "I'm pretty happy where I am, thanks," she said coolly.

"You mentioned wanting to see the world," he tempted. "How about France for starters? You'd feel at home there. I think you'd love the Left Bank. And the shopping! It's better than Rodeo Drive. We could tour the Midi or the Côte d'Azur before we come home. And when we return to California, it would be warm. Wonderful climate we have, no extremes of heat or cold. If we were there now, we could be swimming in the pool. Or surfing in the ocean."

"I can see my organizational and social skills would be strained to the limit," she said ironically. "Somewhere in there between the shopping and surfing, do you plan to make an occasional film?"

"That's why I want to hire you," Wes replied swiftly.

"I'm surprised to hear it, because it was beginning to sound as though you had something else in mind."

Wes realized he had gotten carried away with his inducements. The picture he had begun painting to lure Jennie became so vivid in his mind that he could almost see it himself. "You know what people say. All work and no play... Moviemaking's not a nine-to-five job. There's free time to enjoy as well. I always take a holiday after I finish a film. Sort of a holiday. I'm usually scouting locations or ideas or material, as well. This trip to Montreal is a bit of a holiday," he added.

Jennie was still unconvinced. "If you're really offering me a position, you'd have been wiser to talk about the job, not the fringe benefits."

Wes looked offended. "What did you think I was offering?" he demanded.

"Do all your employees spend their holidays in your personal pool? Do they have access to your car and your art gallery? I don't think so, Mr. Adler." She knew by the flush creeping up from his collar that she was right, and her anger flared higher. "I imagine those dubious privileges are limited to whoever happens to be your lover that season. That would be Blanche this year."

"Blanche isn't my lover!"

"It isn't for lack of trying," she shot back. "You mean the Dom Pérignon and the roses didn't work? Try diamonds. They have a reputation for being a girl's best friend."

"Blanche is a star! She expects those little perks. They're just part of the business."

"And the meetings in her bedroom, where you're not to be interrupted—are they part of the business, too?"

"Yes," he said promptly. "Blanche is very temperamental. Like a baby, really. You have to pamper her, shower her with praise. Her nerves are unsteady. She needs peace and quiet."

"And her director, to hold her hand."

"That's right! Her *director*. That's the only relationship between us. If that's what you're objecting to, Jennie, I can assure you there's nothing more. Never was and never will be. She's not my type."

He sounded earnest, and determined to convince her. Jennie realized the conversation had taken a turn. What did all this matter, anyway, if all he was offering was a job?

"And about the other things I said—the travel, and so on. I was just trying to make the job sound attractive," Wes continued persuasively. "It's actually a tough job. Stars are difficult to work with, demanding, impossible, sometimes. So am I. This wouldn't be easy, but it's the kind of thing you could handle, I think."

Jennie put up her hands to ward him off. "Before you say any more, Wes, I should tell you I'm not at all interested. I like my job very much. I couldn't stand being around Blanche Laure for more than five minutes at a time. Maybe you've got an exaggerated idea of my interpersonal skills. I'm only human."

"I'm not looking for Superwoman," he said reasonably. "Will you think about it at least?"

She shook her head violently. "No, I don't even want to think about it."

Wes gave her a mocking look. "Why? Are you afraid you'd be tempted? You haven't even asked the salary."

Jennie realized her reaction was slightly irrational. Why wouldn't she even think about it? If it was really just a job he was offering... It wasn't the job she wanted, it was the boss. But he wasn't a part of the employment package. She was quiet for a moment, thinking her private thoughts.

Watching her, Wes sensed a weakening. "I might make you an offer you can't refuse," he tempted.

"I doubt it."

"Let's not close the door," he suggested. "Think about it. Not all actors are as demanding as Blanche. Some of them are even nice—honest!"

Jennie smiled reluctantly. "All right, I'll think about it," she said, but her mind was really made up. She just didn't want him to realize why she wouldn't accept. "But remember, I'll be very hard to convince. And now you'd better leave, and let me start drawing up my demands."

Jennie felt a stirring of anger at his reaction. The little smile of triumph, the glitter of success that sparkled in his dark eyes. Did Wescott Adler always get what he wanted? If so, this would be a salutary lesson for him.

He rose without any argument and took his coat.

"I'll call that cab," Jennie said, and went to the phone at once. "It'll be ten minutes," she said, when she hung up. "You might as well wait here for a while. It's cold downstairs."

"Unlike California," he replied with a teasing smile. "I don't plan to waste a single opportunity, you see." He shrugged into his coat. He had less than ten minutes, and quickly figured on how to put it to best advantage. He knew what he wanted to do, but sensed that kissing her wouldn't be wise when he was trying to convince her all he wanted was a new employee.

After an awkward little pause, Jennie said, "I thought you'd be out with Bl—the actors from France tonight."

"I see more than enough of actors. I like to be with real people, when I get the chance. Like you and your friend. Beckie's interesting. It's always nice to meet people with different interests."

"She's very keen on art," Jennie said, and drew the talk about Beckie and art out for a few minutes. She took a peek at her watch. "Maybe you should go downstairs and wait now."

"Yes," he said, but he didn't move. He kept gazing at her, wondering how Jennie had become the way she was. Sure of herself, independent, the kind of woman who didn't need a man to make her life complete. She was one of the very few women he'd met who wasn't impressed with the glitz of Hollywood. She knew what she wanted, and it wasn't that hollow facade of glamour. He felt in his bones she wouldn't change her mind about the job. Maybe he should give a hint of his real reason for offering it.

He wanted an opportunity to know her better, and since he couldn't stay in Montreal, the only other possibility was for her to go with him. Selfish, really, and damned stupid. What if it didn't work out? But as he studied her serious face, he felt in his bones they could work it out. It just needed time, preferably away from work.

After another awkward pause, Jennie said, "What are you and the group doing tomorrow?"

He had to shake himself back to the present. "Blanche will be looking over scripts for her next movie. I'll be meeting with some businessmen, making preparations for my next film. I'm free in the evening. Perhaps we could go somewhere and—talk."

Jennie drew her lower lip between her teeth. She was pulled in two directions by the offer. She would enjoy an ordinary date with Wes, but he'd only try to convince her to work for him. He might even succeed, and she knew that would be sheer folly. It would be torture to watch him pampering his next leading lady. The next one might not be as unlovable as Blanche Laure.

"I think it'd be a waste of time, Wes," she said uncertainly. "My mind's almost made up."

Her answer didn't surprise him. "We could still go out," he said. "Just as friends. You could show me your city. All those things you said you'd show your boyfriend—if you have a boyfriend?" he finished. "Is that why you won't leave?"

"No!" Jennie knew she had answered too quickly, too violently. "No one serious, that is," she added more calmly.

This time he used a more intimate tone. "I don't have a girl, either. In this business, it's hard to meet the kind of woman you'd like to marry." He gazed at her, feeling sure e had met her here, in Montreal. "Jennie—" He was vithin a heartbeat of telling her.

Instead he drew her gently into his arms and kissed her, ust once, lightly on the lips. Then he opened the door and eft.

Jennie found it to be a sad sort of farewell. It felt like goodbye to a lost opportunity. Maybe she should accept is offer. There was definitely a powerful attraction between them, and if he left, she'd never know if it might aave grown into love.

She went to the window and watched him. He had to vait a few minutes for the taxi. When it came, he looked up before he got in. Looking for her apartment, maybe. Of course, he wouldn't know which window was hers in he big building.

Through the sheer curtain, Wes could make out a small orm at one window and smiled softly to himself. Peraaps it was an omen. She was interested enough to have gone to the window to see him off, anyway.

Chapter Eight

When Blanche Laure was having a gown fitted, she didn't go to the couturier. The couturier came to her. As well as Montreal's premier fashion designer, there was a stream of tradesmen trekking up to her suite the next day. They carried boxes and bags containing suits, dresses, sweaters, scarves, shawls, gloves, lingerie and shoes. When Wes returned for lunch, he had one tradesman calling on him, too. His parcel was much smaller. Jennie recognized the man as the manager of one of the finer jewelry stores.

R.K. dropped into her office during the afternoon. She hardly recognized him at first. He had donned a new hairdo and dark suit, and for once he wasn't wearing his sunglasses. Actually, he looked quite handsome.

"I'm after the CEO image," he said, and looked for her reaction.

"By George, you've got it," Jennie told him. "Have you got the job, then?"

"We're still haggling over terms but, in principle, I've got it. If I get the salary I'm after I'll be overpaid, but I'm worth it. That's an old Hollywood joke, J.M.," he explained. "You can laugh."

"So you managed to do whatever it was Wes wanted?" she asked.

"Rightie—right. Time to drop that line. I managed to do what Wes wanted." Jennie looked interested, and he continued.

"You know I have some influence with Blanche. Wes wanted her for another film, and I convinced her she'd be crazy not to take it. It's a marvelous role. A bit of a reach for her, but of course it's only Mother Courage's image that put her off at first. This is not a glamorous part. A poor old bag lady, trudging through Europe during some war or other, peddling her wares from a wagon."

"It's a marvelous role all right," Jennie said. She tried to sound enthusiastic, but she felt as if she'd been betrayed. She had told Wes she would never work with Blanche. He must have had Blanche in mind for this role for ages. That was why he wanted so badly for her to see the play. Why hadn't he told her?

For that matter, why hadn't she suspected? He'd said the next project would be set in France, and he'd talked a lot about *Mother Courage*. He'd said he had to keep Blanche in a good mood, too. Well, Blanche Laure was a big star, of course, and a wonderful actress. She could hardly expect Wes to pass up such an opportunity, just on the chance that she might work for him. The job he'd offered her certainly didn't match Ms. Laure's in importance. But still she felt hurt that he'd kept it a secret. It seemed underhanded.

"Oscar material! No doubt about it," R.K. continued enthusiastically. Bertolt Brecht was no longer passé. "I wouldn't have recommended it to Blanche if I didn't think it was right for her. She's getting a little old for the romantic leads. This is her chance to become a character actress of the first magnitude. It's a gutsy role, something Blanche can really sink her teeth into."

"It's already been made into a movie, hasn't it?" Jennie asked.

"Yes, but quite a while ago. This will be a new interpretation, probably with some feminist overtones, if I know Blanche. And I do. How are your negotiations with Wes progressing, J.M.?"

"They're not. I'm not interested," she said, very firmly.

R.K. rolled his eyes up in disbelief. "It takes all kinds. I was looking forward to working with you in France. And once we get home, we would have a ball in L.A. Wes has a huge house. He throws great parties."

"Hollywood parties, you mean?" she asked cynically.

"Are you kidding? He hates that Hollywood jazz. Occasionally, a big do for his staff. But he prefers entertaining his friends in more intimate situations. He really prefers people outside of the industry. He doesn't go in for that phony tinsel."

"They say that under all the phony tinsel of Hollywood, you find the real tinsel," she said, still cynical. Despite her resolution, she felt tempted by R.K.'s description.

"Yeah, we're all sex fiends and dope addicts. Don't you believe it. Do we seem that way to you?"

Jennie wasn't so sure about R.K., but she certainly thought he was a good person and she was glad to hear he led a reasonable life-style. But she still didn't intend to quit her job to work for him.

"Of course not," she said politely.

"You'll get a taste of the excitement at the premiere tomorrow night. A lot of big names are flying in. Is it true you're going with Mr. Simon?"

Jennie frowned. "Wes promised me two tickets and I told Mr. Simon I'd give him one, but he didn't say anything about accompanying me. I guess it'll be all right to go alone?"

"Tell you what, J.M. You can decorate my arm. I don't have a date. I'll drop Simon's ticket off now. Why don't I give him a pair, and let him know he can bring a date? Is that okay with you?"

"That would be terrific, R.K. I wasn't looking forward to going with him, but I thought at the time he'd like to go." She didn't mention that he'd lost his enthusiasm since the early days. "I guess this will be a formal evening, long gown, the works?"

"A drop-dead gown is definitely required. And maybe you could unbraid your hair for the occasion. I'm kind of curious to see you with it down."

"Don't worry. I won't disgrace you by appearing with straw in my hair," she laughed. "And now you better get out of here and let me get some work done."

"Where do I pick you up?"

"I'll bring my dress here and change, to make it easier."

"Great. I've gotta go and discuss my new salary with Wes while he's in a good mood about Blanche taking the role. You should hear the deal she got. Enough money to retire, plus some nifty perks—like a diamond as big as the Ritz."

"Is that what the jeweler was doing here?" she asked in surprise.

R.K. gave her a peculiar look, almost a guilty look. "I think I've just spoken out of turn. I didn't say that, okay?"

"What do you mean?"

"I just thought maybe Wes wouldn't like me telling you about the diamond ring he gave Blanche."

"It has nothing to do with me," she said swiftly, but she felt disappointed just the same. A diamond ring wasn't just an expensive piece of jewelry. It had a well-known traditional meaning. "Are they engaged or something?" she asked, trying to sound indifferent.

"Good lord no! At least I don't think so. My God, he wouldn't go *that* far to get her for the film, would he? No, I'm sure it's just a present, a little bonus. Wes is generous to his employees. He's always presenting his star with little trinkets at the close of a project. This time it's more ostentatious because he was after her for *Mother Courage*, as well. I told you, when Wes wants something, he doesn't spare any trouble or expense. He's one stubborn old son-of-a-gun. I bet he'll win you over, too, J.M.," he said, laughing.

"Don't put any money on it," she said firmly.

R.K. finally left, but Jennie found it hard to get back to work. If Wes had hidden from her that he was hiring Blanche for his next movie, maybe he'd been devious about other things—like being Blanche's lover. Maybe he'd even had R.K. come in to tell her what a great guy he was . . . R.K. wanted that job very badly.

She shook herself back to reality. She was getting carried away here. Wes wouldn't go to that much trouble just to hire an employee. He probably wouldn't even do that to get a new mistress, even if he was a stubborn son-of-a-gun. She managed to push the ugly thought out of her mind and get some work done. The major gala at the hotel was the party following the movie premiere the next evening. There were dozens of details to keep track of there, and she was soon caught up in her work.

She wasn't even thinking of Wes, when he dropped into her office around five. He had come in from outdoors, and his face was ruddy from the cold. The wind had whipped his hair awry and his nose was red, but he was still dangerously attractive. He wore that intangible aura of confidence that success confers. It wasn't any one thing she could put her finger on, but a combination of posture and attitude and facial expression that spelled power.

"Hi, Jen. Are we on for tonight?" he asked.

Nothing had been settled about that date. The temptation was there. She steeled herself against it and said "I'm afraid not," just glancing up briefly from her work.

He walked close to her desk but didn't sit down. "No strings. Just a couple of friends, seeing the town together," he said.

The word friend conjured up that moment of sadness when he had left her last night. It had wrenched her heart painfully. And the parting would be more painful if she went on seeing him. She took a deep breath, crossed her fingers below her desk and said, "I'm up to my eyeballs in work, Wes. The premiere..."

"Doesn't the hotel have a night concierge to take over?"

"No, it's just a small hotel. The desk clerk acts as manager. If anything critical comes up, he phones Mr. Simon or me."

She thought he'd leave. He sat down and threw one long leg over the other, settling in for a while. "What do you have to do? Maybe I can help. After all, it's my premiere."

As there was really no crushing load of unfinished work, Jennie said uncertainly, "Just details. It's my problem."

He put both hands flat on the desk. The determined angle of his chin told her he was going to be hard to dissuade. "I'm good at details," he said. "Let's get it done with. You lay the problem on me, and we'll thrash it out together. Okay, what's the first?"

Jennie decided his reputation for stubbornness was well earned. He didn't intend to leave, and she was equally determined to get rid of him. "I'll handle it," she said, becoming annoyed.

The sharp edge in her voice made him wary. When he looked at her fiery eyes and rigid chin, he suspected the work was just an excuse. His temper began to rise.

"I like people who come out and say what what's on their mind," he said curtly. "If you don't want to go out with me, just tell me. The work is an excuse—right?"

"Yes, it's an excuse. Not that I need one. I told you in the beginning I don't date clients."

"It didn't stop you before," he reminded her swiftly.

"Well, it's stopping me now. And furthermore, I didn't date you. You followed me to the museum."

"You went to the play on your own. You knew I'd be there, in the next seat."

There was no answer to that charge, so Jennie attacked on a different front. "Funny you didn't tell me why you were there. What was the great secret about *Mother Courage* being your next film? Or was it just the leading lady you wanted to keep under wraps?"

A quick blaze of frustration faded quickly. She could almost see the gears grind as he decided to admit it, and try to explain. "So that's it! Until the deal was down, I didn't tell anyone, to avoid competition. I don't think it's my choice of film that's got you upset. You're angry that I hired Blanche, when I knew you didn't like working with her. I'd been working on that deal for a year, Jennie. It'll be a great project, and Blanche is the only one to play the role."

"But why didn't you tell me? You would have let me quit my job, then I'd be stuck working for her."

Wes ran his hand through his tousled hair. "I don't know. I knew you'd refuse if I told you. I didn't want you to refuse."

"So you hid it from me. That's a sneaky, underhanded thing to do. I'd never work for someone like that."

He sensed her outrage and knew it was justified, but felt impotent to soothe it. "I didn't want—" He bit the words off. "You wouldn't have had much to do with Blanche. She's my department—and R.K.'s. He can handle her pretty well."

"Not as well as you can. Of course, he can't afford to shower her with diamonds."

"The diamond wasn't for—!" He came to an abrupt stop. "It wasn't a diamond. It was a star sapphire. A bonus."

"For what, Wes? She's treated like a queen. Her salary's stupendous, I hear. Is the bonus for compliance above the call of duty?"

His body went perfectly rigid, and when he spoke his voice was light with disbelief. "Are you accusing me of buying her sexual favors? Is that it?"

"I'm not accusing. I'm just asking a question. And since I don't really give a damn what you give her, or why, you needn't answer."

"I don't have to ask who your informant was," he said stiffly. His eyes were snapping, and Jennie was afraid for R.K.

The name R.K. Benson, though unspoken, hung in the air between them. Jennie remembered too late that he'd asked her not to mention the ring. In the heat of battle, she'd gotten carried away. But since it was out she couldn't very well deny it. "More secrets?" she asked, with a sneer.

"If you want the whole truth, it's all your fault!" Wes said, and sat glaring at her. His hand went to his pocket. But this was so obviously the wrong time to tell the truth that he drew it out empty. "Jennie, we've got to talk."

"I don't think we have anything more to say to each other," she snapped, and pulled a paper toward her to show the conversation was over.

"I think we have a great deal to say." He reached out and removed the paper, then held her fingers. His dark eyes gazed into hers, not arrogantly but almost beseechingly, and she found her breath catching in her throat. "The customer's always right," he said, and she allowed him to help her up from her chair. "Let's get out of here. This office is too public." He held his arm loosely around her waist as they went toward the door, causing her some emotional turmoil. "It's your town. Where can we go to be alone?" he asked.

"I can't walk out on a busy day like this!" she exclaimed. What was she doing, letting her heart rule her head like this? She was letting Wes Adler interfere with her duties, which was completely against her principles.

"Then we'll stay in the hotel and go to the bar—after all, I am a client. And you know us movie folks. If it's not one vice, it's another."

With this sop of his being a client, she let him carry her off to the bar, though she felt in her bones that this meeting had little to do with work. The bar was busy at five o'clock with the office crowd stopping in for some relaxation before going home. Bodies jostled between the crowded tables, and a hubbub of raised voices nearly drowned out conversation.

"Isn't there anywhere else we could go?" Wes asked, frowning. He didn't want a crowd for what he had to say but didn't like to suggest his room, in case Jennie misinterpreted his intentions.

"Crowds provide a kind of privacy," she said, and pointed to an empty table in a nice secluded corner. "I'm going to relax my rule and have a drink, even if I am still on duty."

She ordered a wine cooler and settled in for some private talk. The first item of importance was to exonerate R.K. "Wes, I don't want you to think R.K. intentionally told me about your hiring Blanche for your next picture. He thought I already knew."

Wes batted the detail away with a flick of his hand. He didn't want to waste this interlude talking about R.K. "You would have had to know, sooner or later. About Blanche, Jennie, it's not what you think. We're just fellow colleagues, and friends."

She gave him a leery look. "That must be a unique situation. I don't imagine Blanche has many disinterested male friends."

"Very true. She doesn't have any, except me. She's partly to blame, I admit. She does love to play the shining star, but underneath the glitz and glamour, there's a lonely lady—not even trying very hard to get out. I don't think she even realizes she's lonesome, because she's so often surrounded by people. You mentioned when we came in here that there's a kind of privacy in a crowd. There can be loneliness in a crowd, too. Most of those people want something from her."

"And she wants something from them, too, I think," Jennie added bluntly.

"It's known as give and take. They want to trade in on her name. She knows that the harder she makes it for them, the better she'll be treated."

"She sounds like an egomaniac," Jennie said, still not convinced.

"More insecure than anything else. Haven't you noticed the insecure ones seem to need constant reassuring?"

Jennie gave him a sharp glance. Was he still talking about Blanche, or had he included her now? "She has nothing to be insecure about."

"Actresses are the most insecure people on earth. They have to prove themselves every time out. Blanche is only as good as her last picture. And as the beauty begins to fade..." He just hunched his shoulders.

"You make her sound like a monument," Jennie objected.

"She is a monument of cinema. I remember sitting in the theater when I was sixteen or so, watching her movies. She seemed bigger than life to me. It was like a dream come true when I got a chance to direct her. I felt so—inadequate. But she made it easy. She wasn't terribly confident, either. She depended totally on her director, and together we remade her career and made mine. I owe her a lot, Jennie. I don't dump my friends. I owe her, especially now that's she's no longer young. How can you despise a woman so desperate for real affection when the only thing reciprocating it is a dog? You can only feel pity for her, try to help her. She's a great actress. She has a lot to give, and she gives one hundred percent where it counts—in front of a camera. I admire Blanche's talent and professionalism. I even like her, warts and all, but I'm not in love her."

"I can't deny her talent," Jennie said pensively.

"And you don't have to worry that I'm romantically involved with her, in spite of the sapphire ring."

She felt rather foolish. What right did she have to question Wes's relationship with his leading lady? From what he said, it was fifty percent pity and fifty percent admiration of her acting. He was probably the only real friend Blanche had. It took a man of understanding to see beneath Blanche's bristly facade and find some redeeming qualities. "It's none of my business, anyway," she said.

"I have no objection if you'd like to *make* it your business," Wes said encouragingly. He gave her a perfectly devastating smile. It started as an intimate glow in his eyes, which lingered there as a warm blush crept up her neck. It slowly possessed his face, softening the rugged contours, gently easing his lips apart. She wanted to look away, but felt mesmerized. His fingers closed over hers and squeezed, all the time keeping a gaze on her, as if she were some rare and cherished jewel.

She felt as if she had been thoroughly kissed. Her whole body was aglow. There was a noticeable pause before she felt capable of speaking, then she could think of nothing to say. When she finally spoke, her voice was breathless and her words perfectly inane. "It's really quite private here, in this corner, isn't it?" she said.

"Not private enough to suit me." He squeezed her fingers harder, then released them. "We were talking about you making my business your business," he reminded her.

Jennie gave a nervous laugh. "How did we get on that subject?" She reached for her glass.

Wes took her other hand, her left hand, and began massaging her fingers. "One thing led to another," he said. "And who knows what 'another' will lead to?"

His stroking fingers had settled on the third finger of her left hand. Jennie wondered if he realized it. There was an old wives' tale that that particular finger was chosen for the wedding ring because it was connected directly to the heart. At that moment, she could believe it. She could almost feel the tug at her heart as his fingers moved possessively over hers.

"How long have you known Blanche?" she asked, in an effort to retain a shred of sanity.

"Seven years. Why are we talking about Blanche, again? I've explained all that."

"Seven years—that's good luck, isn't it? Or is it bad luck? If you break a mirror—" She was babbling, and came to a halt.

"She hasn't broken a mirror," he said.

"Not yet."

"Then we can resume our former topic. Business— mine, hopefully becoming yours."

His fingers still clung to her left hand, disturbing her with impossible ideas of eternal love. For a crazy minute, Jennie had the idea it wasn't business he was talking about at all. His penetrating gaze demanded something more from her than that. The temptation to give in was overwhelmingly strong. Life would be a roller coaster as Wes's personal secretary. The first phase, she knew, would whirl her straight up into the giddy heights of bliss. But when he lost interest in her, when he grew tired of whatever novelty she brought to his life, what then? Would she dwindle into a female version of R.K.? A shallow woman, worrying about her hair and clothes.

She raised her chin up, her resolve firmed, and said, "Sorry, Wes. I'm not the type."

"I disagree, Ms. Longman," he said firmly. "You are exactly the type I want." Wes flicked a quick, impatient look around the restaurant, wondering if the crowd provided enough privacy for a proposal. Popping the question in this place was certainly too public for the passionate embrace that would accompany it.

"I'm no yes-woman," she warned.

"I've noticed!" His sharp rejoinder was accompanied by a rueful laugh. "I have definitely noticed that tendency to say no—almost before you've heard the question."

She tilted her head to one side. "Then it won't come as any surprise when I say it again."

"You've never let me outline my—proposal," he said, deliberating over the last word. He caught the gleam of interest that flashed over her animated face. His hand went to his pocket, caressing the small box there.

"Whatever it is, the answer's still no. No, no, no." Jennie heard the edge of desperation in her objection, suddenly feeling the urge to run away. Because if she stayed, she feared she'd give in to his persuasions. She pushed her glass aside and reached for her purse.

"Wait!" Wes's hand fell like a vice on her arm. "We'll go up to my room."

In a pig's eye she would! Before she could say no again, they were interrupted. R.K. Benson came rushing up to them, wearing a disheveled look and looking wild eyed. "What's the matter?" Wes demanded in a grim voice.

"Disaster!" R.K. announced, literally pulling his hair. "She's gone! Disappeared from her room."

Wes jumped up, upsetting his drink. His face went pale, and his body became momentarily rigid. He seemed incapable of speech.

Jennie's heart jolted and she jumped up, too. "Ms. Laure?" she asked. What could have happened? Visions of Blanche stomping out in a fit of rage, or being killed in a traffic accident, or kidnapped, flashed before her eyes. Blanche Laure kidnapped from the Mont Royal Hotel. "I'd better tell Mr. Simon."

R.K. looked from Wes to her as if they were both insane. "Not Blanche! Ruby."

Wes's body visibly relaxed. Jennie watched as the look of mute horror left his face. "Why can't she keep that mutt tied up?" he growled, and strode angrily out the door.

Jennie's pounding heart slowed to a thud. She had seen how Wes reacted to his fear for Blanche's safety. Whatever he might say, and maybe even believe, he was deeply involved with her. She didn't think anything but love could have made him so worried. And even Blanche's dog took preference over herself, she noticed. So much for the giddy heights of romance!

Chapter Nine

Jennie shook her mind back to attention and said to Benson, "Ruby must be around the hotel somewhere. How long has she been missing?" She made a quick decision not to tell Mr. Simon. It was probably just a tempest in a teapot, and he was already distressed enough with the Olympia guests.

"We haven't a clue. She was with Blanche when I left her to come here earlier this afternoon. Blanche has been very busy, with people coming and going. The door's been open a dozen times. Ruby must have slipped out unnoticed. Blanche is having a full-blown fit of hysterics. We've got to do something."

"I'll notify the staff and have them search the hotel," Jennie said. R.K. followed her to her office. She began pushing phone buttons and issuing orders. "Why don't you help the search?" she suggested.

"I'd better go back to Blanche. Call a doctor, will you? Maybe a psychiatrist—I don't know." He straggled out of the office.

Jennie made a call to the hotel doctor. Perhaps he could prescribe a tranquilizer or sleeping pill, to calm the woman. She sat a moment thinking. She wanted to wallow in her own hurt and disappointment, but her mind overruled. Where was the likeliest place a dog would go? A dog was led by its nose. Maybe the kitchen . . . She reached for the phone, but it rang before she could complete her call.

"The concierge's office. Ms. Longman speaking," she said.

"This is Blanche Laure. I want you upstairs immediately."

Jennie bristled at the arrogant tone. If that lady was insecure, the Pope was an atheist. Before she could reply, the receiver clicked loudly in her ear. "Immediately," as if she were Blanche Laure's slave. Every atom of her body rebelled at the idea, but she looked at her certificate from Les Clefs d'Or on the wall and swallowed her anger.

Within two minutes, she tapped on Blanche's door. It was thrown open and she was confronted by the impressive sight of Blanche Laure in the midst of one of her infamous towering rages. Her cascading hair and the flame red dressing gown trailing behind her lent drama to her performance.

"It took you long enough!" she exclaimed, and pulled Jennie in by the wrist. Jennie noticed that Wes was in the room, looking under the bed. With one hand on her hip, Blanche threw her other hand into the air and went into her spiel.

"I have never, in all my years of travel, visited such a careless establishment as this. *No* facilities provided for guests! The food tasteless, the service abominable, the weather something only an Eskimo could enjoy, and now *this*! You've allowed Ruby to be kidnapped.''

Jennie listened, and when Blanche stopped for a breath she said, ''How long has she been missing?''

''How should I know? She was here this afternoon.'' She looked over her shoulder to Wes, just getting up from the floor. Her voice lowered an octave and the vibrato increased. ''The poor little thing. She'll freeze in this climate. She's practically hairless, and she wasn't even wearing her sweater.''

''Has she disappeared before?'' Jennie asked.

Blanche threw a hand over her forehead and swooped in a distracted circle. ''Once, in Hawaii. She was found by a surfer on the beach. She likes water.''

''She won't find any unfrozen here,'' Jennie said curtly. ''I'll go to the kitchen. That seems the likeliest attraction.''

''If you can call the food served here an attraction,'' Blanche snipped. ''In fact, if you can call what comes out of that kitchen food—''

''Our cuisine is famous, Ms. Laure. We're four-star in the *Michelin Guide*.''

''Poor Ruby,'' Blanche said, ignoring the comment. ''Perhaps we'd better call in the police, Wes. Would you darling?'' She reached out her long arm, grasping his hand.

''It's a bit early for that, Blanche,'' he said. ''Let's have a thorough search of the hotel first. I'll go with Ms. Longman.''

''If Ruby's been missing for hours, maybe I should call the dog pound,'' Jennie said, and used Blanche's phone to do it.

Blanche shivered in revulsion. "My poor baby, locked up like a criminal. I'll offer a reward. Anything!"

Jennie didn't mention the reward. The dog catchers were municipal employees. Offering a reward would have been inappropriate. Ruby hadn't been found, so she left the hotel number to call if she turned up.

"Let me know the instant you hear anything," Blanche said in her throbbing vibrato.

"Certainly, Ms. Laure," Jennie replied.

"You called a doctor for me?"

"He's on his way. Try not to worry. I'm sure we'll find Ruby," she said, and walked out of the room. Wes followed her.

"You'd think it was a child, the way she carries on," she scolded as they went down the hall, tapping on doors.

"Blanche has no children. Ruby means a lot to her."

A disgruntled man opened his door at their knock and Jennie explained their errand.

"A chihuahua?" he asked. "I thought no dogs were allowed in this hotel. The whole place is going to the dogs if you ask me. You won't get my business again. The halls full of tradesmen. Doors slamming. Music playing. If I wanted noise and confusion, I'd have gone to Coney Island."

"I'm very sorry to have disturbed you, Mr. Carney," Jennie said.

"It's Blanche Laure's dog," Wes added. "She's next door. I'm sorry if the traffic disturbed you."

"Blanche Laure? The movie star!" Mr. Carney's face lit up like a Christmas tree. "You mean she's right next door to me?" He took a step into the hall and glanced reverently down at her closed door. "I'll slip on my shoes and help you look for the dog," he said eagerly.

Jennie's blood simmered. Was the whole world in love with Blanche? She could do no wrong. She was Blanche Laure.

Wes shrugged. "I thought it might be good for PR. It prevented you from losing a guest to Coney Island."

"Thanks," she said curtly.

Two hotel maids got off the elevator and Jennie spoke to them. "Rap on every door," she said. "And be sure you apologize for disturbing the guests. If there's no answer on the third rap, use your key. Ruby could have slipped in when a maid was making the bed and got locked in," she explained to Wes.

"Is it true the dog belongs to Blanche Laure?" one of the maids asked, wide-eyed.

"Yes," Wes smiled, "and she wants to personally thank whoever finds it."

With a signed photo, Jennie added mentally. The girls chattered excitedly and hurried on their way.

"If the maids are checking the rooms, maybe we should look somewhere else," he said.

"You can go back to Blanche if you want. We'll handle this."

He gave her a disparaging look. "Do you think I'm a masochist! I'll help you look."

"You might try the kitchen," Jennie suggested. "I'll go to the laundry. Ruby could have gotten herself tied up in a load of laundry during the cleaning. I'll check the supply cupboards too."

Wes didn't heed her hint to go to the kitchen. He followed along while Jennie unlocked the supply room door to look around. Shelves rose up from floor to ceiling.

"You don't have to climb shelves," Wes said. "If Ruby were here, you'd hear her."

"I'm going to walk down the fire exit to the basement," Jennie said. "The stairs are one place she could
bark her head off and no one would hear."

She set a fast pace, flying down the stairs with her high
heels clicking on the concrete. She opened the door on
every landing to see that the employees were still assisting
with the search. They went on to the kitchen.

Pierre smiled when she entered. "Jennie! I must be in
hot water if you've come in person. What have I done
wrong? Was Ms. Laure's afternoon tea not to her liking?
She asked for Soo Chong. I had to send a *garçon* out to
buy it, so don't yell at me if it took half an hour."

"You never do anything wrong, Pierre. You're just
fishing for compliments. You know you're the best chef
in Montreal," Jennie said, and stated her errand.

Wes listened, admiring the way she handled the situation. She soothed feathers as she went, and didn't use a
crisis as an excuse for bad manners. There was no bedlam but a smooth, organized effort, optimizing the hotel's resources. She hadn't even lost her temper with the
impossible Blanche.

Ruby wasn't in the kitchen. She wasn't in the laundry
room. The Mont Royal was an old hotel, and had its own
in-house laundry facilities. Jennie phoned the house-
keeper from the laundry, and learned that Ruby was still
missing.

"We might as well check out the rest of the basement
while we're here," she said. "It's kind of grungy down
here, Wes. Why don't you go upstairs and look around?
Or maybe outside—Ruby might have gone off the prem-
ises, you know."

"She'd soon come back again once she felt the arctic
air. Ruby hates the cold weather. My bet is we'll find her
tucked up asleep in front of some heater."

"Couldn't she have gotten into your room? She might have headed to some place she's familiar with," Jennie said. She noticed Wes stiffened at the inquiry.

"She's not familiar with my room. Blanche has never been there, with or without Ruby."

Discussing the relationship between Wes and his star was the farthest thing from Jennie's mind when she asked the question. She sidestepped it now by saying, "I wonder if anyone else in the hotel is traveling with a dog. That would be an attraction. No, I'm sure they're not," she said, after mentally reviewing the clients.

"Where is this store room?" Wes asked. Jennie turned, leading him down a dusty flight of stairs, into the bowels of the building.

She pushed a switch, and unshaded lights created puddles of illumination in the darkness. There were no plush carpets or chandeliers or marble here, nothing but rough, exposed beams and a concrete floor. Stacks of discarded furniture were ranged along the wall, covered with tarpaulins. It wasn't cold, but it was chilly enough to be uncomfortable. Wes whistled and called a few times.

"She's not here," he decided.

"There's a corridor that leads to the wine cellar. We might as well make the complete tour since we've come this far," Jennie said.

The door was locked, but the keys on her heavy chain were labeled, and she was able to get in. Before them stretched rows of racks with the bottles tilted to keep the cork wet.

"Wow! Wouldn't I love to own this!" Wes exclaimed, and took a few steps forward to check some labels.

"The good stuff's over there," Jennie said, indicating a far corner. Wes went to glance at a few bottles. "Our reds are mostly French, but we have some German white wines. We even have a small cache of Médoc, Chateau Lafite, Rothschild.''

"I didn't see *that* on the wine list!"

"It costs a fortune. The only time it's been served since I've been here was when the premiere of France visited. We keep the temperature low for the wine, between fifty and fifty-five, so Ruby wouldn't have fallen asleep here. Let's go.''

"Any other ideas?'' Wes asked.

"I'm going upstairs to check. Someone might have found her by now.''

They went up to the lobby. Mr. Simon was just coming from Jennie's office. He looked distracted with worry. "Oh, there you are! I've been looking all over for you, Ms. Longman. What's the idea of trying to hide this latest development from me? It seems that you let Ms. Laure's dog escape?''

"I wasn't in charge of it! It escaped from her room.''

"You should have notified me at once. If Benson hadn't told me what happened, I'd still be in the dark.''

"I was just trying to spare you the aggravation. I thought we'd find the dog before now.''

"And did you?'' he demanded, in a purely rhetorical spirit.

"No. The entire staff is out scouring the hotel.''

"The hotel has been scoured. It's not here. You should have notified me at once, Ms. Longman.''

Wes was angry at his attack on Jennie. He had to defend her. "And what would you have done, Mr. Simon?'' he asked.

Mr. Simon gave him a quick, flustered glare. "I would have handled the situation.''

"Ms. Longman has handled it superbly. Every possible step has been taken.''

Wes thought the man looked on the verge of suffering a heart attack, and tried to calm him. "I'm sure Ruby will turn up in some warm, dark corner. We'll keep looking. Don't fret yourself."

Simon turned on him. "That's easy for you to say. Your job isn't on the line."

"It's hardly that crucial, Mr. Simon."

"The hell it isn't. Ms. Laure's called in the police, if you please! She's calling it a dognapping. It'll be all over the papers by tomorrow. If Benson hadn't warned me, we would have had the hotel full of uniformed men. Fortunately I was able to contact the police department, asking them to send plainclothesmen. The board will still have me on the carpet for this. I rue the day I ever let this bunch of—" His flaming eye fell on Adler, and he choked back whatever outrageous description he had in mind for the Olympia group.

"I'll be in my office," Mr. Simon said to Jennie. "You won't be leaving before the dog is found, Ms. Longman."

It sounded more like a command than a question. "Of course," she said.

Wes found himself receiving a baleful glare from Jennie. "You don't have to try to protect me. I can look after myself," she said angrily.

"You shouldn't have let him blame you. It's not your fault."

"It is, partly. I should have notified him. That was an error in judgment. I'm glad he got through to the police in time to request plainclothes officers. He didn't mean what he said to me. He's just upset. I bet Blanche did it on purpose. She just wants the publicity."

It was Wes's turn to poker up with a glare. "Don't be ridiculous. Blanche doesn't have to resort to cheap stunts

like this. She can have all the free publicity she wants by
simply lifting the telephone. She's refused more interviews than she's given since we've been here. I've had to
give her hell to make her cooperate."

"Hell? I thought it was jewelry you gave her. Maybe
this stunt is *your* idea, Mr. Adler. You don't seem very
concerned over Ruby's disappearance." But you were
certainly concerned when you thought it was Blanche who
had disappeared, she thought.

"I'll blame that insult on your nerves. Don't take it out
on *me* because your boss ripped into you. If you had any
pride, you'd quit after what he said."

"And go to work for you, you mean? No thanks. A
week of Blanche Laure is more than enough for me."

She turned and stalked to her office. She was too agi-
tated to sit down, so she paced, trying to think, through
the miasma of anger and hurt. Mr. Simon was impossible. He knew it wasn't her fault. Of course, he'd apologize, but she wished he hadn't ripped up in front of Wes.
She was furious with Wes, and with herself for having lost
her cool. Most of all she was exasperated with Blanche
Laure, just for being Blanche.

What could she do? Improvise, Mr. Simon would say,
but how did you improvise your way out of a dognapping that would bring unfavorable publicity to the Mont
Royal? The first order of business had to be finding that
dog, then they would have to invent an explanation that
countered the bad publicity. Something to exonerate the
hotel and, of course, something that didn't reflect badly
on Ms. Laure.

Her phone rang. It was Mr. Simon. "The police are
here. Just thought you'd like to know. They've gone up
to Laure's suite. About what I said before, Ms. Longman. I'm sorry. Nerves, you know." Mr. Simon always

apologized by phone. He was actually rather shy. "Now that we're all calmer, would you fill me in on what steps you've taken? Adler said you handled it superbly. I'm sure he was right."

She accepted the peace offering and wasted the next few minutes filling Simon in on her efforts.

"It would be funny if it weren't so damned annoying," he said. "Till we find the mutt, I can't quite see the humor in it. Oh well, this too will pass. We'll soon be rid of them all and back to normal bedlam."

He hung up, leaving Jennie with thoughts of what he had just said. Mr. Simon was right. The Olympia group would soon be gone. Jennie suddenly felt a heaviness on her heart.

Chapter Ten

Jennie forgot to eat dinner that evening. She kept abreast of the dognapping by phone and by periodic visits to Mr. Simon's office and the lobby. She unearthed the blueprints of the hotel and examined them for any nook or cranny she might have overlooked. A chihuahua was tiny enough to slide into almost any cavity, and the doorman was quite certain Ruby hadn't escaped. Wes said the dog wouldn't take more than three steps in the snow before going back to the warmth, so it looked as if she was still in the hotel somewhere.

R.K. assured her there hadn't been any demand for payment, so dognapping seemed unlikely. Blanche allowed the doctor to prescribe a tranquilizer, but she put off taking it. She was too busy performing for the police and the media.

At eight-thirty the phone rang, and Jennie grabbed it eagerly.

"It's Wes," the voice on the other end said.

"Have you found Ruby?" she demanded at once.

"No. I thought I should warn you, Jennie, this thing is turning into a media blitz."

"You didn't call the press!"

"I swear on this Gideon I'm holding that I didn't know they were doing it. My PR boys did it without asking me. Well, promotion is their job. I've always encouraged them to use their initiative, and this is a natural. It also brings a lot of attention to tomorrow's opening of *Orphan*."

"You said all Blanche had to do to get publicity was lift the phone. I still think she arranged the whole thing." As soon as she said it, Jennie realized this would infuriate Wes, but she was beyond caring.

His mild answer surprised her. "It occurred to me, but Blanche does seem genuinely disturbed. She's quiet, which means she isn't acting. And, incidentally, it isn't just the press. The TV crews are coming too. It'll probably be on the wire all across America. I see it grabbing at least one magazine cover."

"Oh, lord. Simon will have a heart attack."

"I don't know what's bothering him. It'll put his little hotel on the map," Wes said reasonably.

"The Mont Royal doesn't want to be on *that* map! We're a discreet, low-key establishment."

"Then why did you ever let us in?" he asked with a little laugh. "You must have known Blanche always grabs headlines."

"It isn't funny, Wes. I've got to go. Thanks for warning me."

"What are you doing?"

"Worrying."

"I'll come down to help you. R.K. can stay with Blanche and meet the media."

The phone clicked, and Jennie hung up the receiver. She dampened the thrill of knowing Wes was coming to her. It was strictly business, at least that was the way she meant to keep it. She turned her attention back to the blueprints, concentrating on the heating system. When Wes entered, he found her puzzling over the papers, frowning in an effort to understand them. Jennie looked pale and tired and harried. She was taking all this much too seriously. He wanted to tell her so, but he knew she'd resent it. He also wanted to take her in his arms and say, "There, there. It's going to be all right." He didn't think she'd appreciate that, either.

"What have you got there?" he asked, walking toward the desk to look over her shoulder.

Jennie just glanced up when he spoke. She was careful not to smile, but she couldn't quite control the gleam in her eyes. "Plans for the hotel," she said. "I thought I might discover some warm little corner where Ruby may be hiding out."

"Let's follow the heat ducts," he suggested, using it as an excuse to stand close to her. Their shoulders brushed as he inclined his head toward hers. A flowery scent wafted toward him. It suited her. Blanche's cloying musk perfume had always been overpowering to Wes.

Jennie was acutely aware of his hovering warmth. When he put one arm over her shoulder to trace the heat pipes with his finger, she could feel his breath gently fan her ear and cheek. A ripple of pleasure surged through her.

"The heat is vented to the rooms and the hall," she pointed out in a very businesslike manner. "We searched the rooms. In the hall, there's nothing Ruby could hide behind or under. The grates are in plain view, so she can't be there. The only other thing I can think of is food. What time does she usually eat?''

"She was due for her bowl at four or five. She should be ravenous by now, but we checked the kitchen.''

Jennie threw up her hands. "It's hopeless. I can't think of anything else.''

"I didn't think you were a quitter!'' Wes challenged.

Jennie's head whipped around to glare at him. "I'm not,'' she said firmly.

His face was only inches from hers. She could distinguish the individual hairs in his lashes; beyond them she could see the myriad, opalescent tints in the depth of his dove gray eyes. She felt uncomfortable with him hovering over her, especially when the challenge was softening to something else. Jennie stood up suddenly, in an awkward movement that revealed her feelings.

Wes just went on looking, wearing a peculiar little smile now. It was impossible to read what he was thinking. "You don't have much imagination,'' he said, in his calm way. "Warmth and food aren't the only basic animal needs. There's company. To be blunt, sex. Maybe Ruby was lonesome for some canine companionship.''

"You would think of that!'' she retorted, angrily, for no sane reason.

"We're all part animal, aren't we? I've merely tried to put myself in Ruby's place. If you spent your life surrounded by dogs, wouldn't you occasionally want to be with a human being?''

Jennie made an effort to recover her equilibrium and said, "It makes sense, I guess. But there aren't any other dogs at the hotel. We made an exception in Blanche's case.''

"The sex drive is strong. It might have propelled Ruby out to the world beyond the hotel,'' he suggested.

"You said the cold would keep her inside! She wouldn't go more than three steps."

Wes hunched his shoulders. "I could be wrong."

"I'm surprised to hear you admit it. If she's gotten out, we'll never find her."

His smile stretched to a mocking grin. "Never? That sounds like a quitter's remark. Normally, Ruby hates the cold. It'd take some special enticement to lure her out of her comfortable hotel niche. Maybe some enterprising little hound dog led her off to his warm lair. Do you ever see any dogs around the neighborhood?"

That was the second time he'd called her a quitter. She wouldn't stop the search now if it took a year. She thought about his question objectively. Forget that he was teasing her with all this talk of sex, drawing some parallel to herself with that "comfortable hotel niche" crack, and concentrate on the problem at hand. She said, "We don't see many dogs off the leash in this area. It's a commercial district. Although—" She stopped. "I have occasionally seen cats prowling around the rear of the building where the trash is put out. The garbage cans have even been knocked over a few times."

"That sounds like dogs!" Wes said. He grabbed her coat and threw it over her shoulders. "Let's go."

"You can't go out without a coat. It's freezing."

A spark of mischief flashed in his eyes. "We can share your fur."

"We'll borrow Mr. Simon's coat," she decided. He wasn't in his office, so she just took it from the rack and Wes put it on. It looked quite ludicrous, pulled tightly across his wide chest with two inches of bare wrist sticking out at the bottom.

"Nice scarf," he said, taking a plaid muffler, too.

Unfortunately, they met Mr. Simon in the hallway. He was in another fit of vapors. "Now she's called in the newspapers and TV crews," he complained. "The hotel is crawling with cameramen and reporters. I might as well write my resignation and save myself the ignominy of being fired. Where are you going, Ms. Longman?"

"Just checking out another idea."

"And why are you wearing my coat?" he demanded of Wes.

"I left mine upstairs. Do you mind?"

"Well! Oh, go on, if it will help find that little—dog," he said, choking back the word mongrel. "But take care of the coat. It's cashmere."

"It's very nice," Wes said.

Mr. Simon smiled in surprise. "Yes, it is rather."

The route to the back door was through the kitchen. Wes and Jennie ran downstairs into Pierre's steaming, warm domain. The tempting aromas wafting there reminded Jennie she had skipped dinner.

"Sorry for the intrusion, Pierre. We're just going out to check the garbage cans."

"Did you find Ruby?" Pierre asked.

"Not yet."

"Bring her to me when you do. I'll prepare her special dish." He already had the silver bowl out on the table.

The rear of the hotel opened into an alley that led to the street. The garbage cans were kept just outside the door until garbage day. The hotel generated a lot of waste, twenty large bins so far that week. They were all tidily covered except one, that had been tipped over. The plastic bag inside was torn open and some scraps littered the ground. A shadow slunk away as they approached, giving temporary hope, but it was only a cat, approximately the size and color of Ruby.

"That must have been done by a dog," Jennie said, looking at the tipped bins. "But Ruby's too small to have done it. She could hardly knock over a teacup. I'll tell Pierre to have it cleaned up."

"Let's just lift lids, to be positive Ruby's not here," Wes suggested, and began doing so immediately.

Jennie started at the other end of the row and met him in the middle. "My career has struck a new low—rummaging through garbage cans," she said glumly.

Wes turned, smiling down at her apologetically. "All the fault of those yahoos from Hollywood. I'm damned sorry, Jennie."

She was tired and depressed and in no mood to argue. "It's all right. I'm sure you aren't enjoying this any more than I am."

"You're wrong there. I am enjoying it—sort of. Of course, the ambience isn't exactly roses and moonbeams, but it did bring us together."

Jennie felt, again, that sad tugging at her heart. She glanced up at the sky. A cold white moon floated in the infinity of blackness. It looked lonesome, the way she felt. In some perverse way she was missing Wes, and he hadn't even left yet.

She lifted her pale face and examined the sky. "Actually there are moonbeams," she pointed out, rather wistfully. "And probably plenty of roses, too, in the garbage cans. There must be. Blanche gets dozens of them," she added less wistfully.

The very thought of that woman was enough to harden Jennie's mood. "It's freezing here. Let's go inside," she said, turning to leave.

Wes stopped her, putting a hand on her arm. There was no mocking or teasing or smiling now. His voice sounded a little sad, the way Jennie felt. "I guess this really clinches it, huh? You'd never consider working for me now."

"I never was seriously considering it. I like doing what I do," she said pugnaciously.

"You do it very well. I was just needling you when I called you a quitter. I felt you needed a shot of adrenaline. Competitive people like us always respond to a challenge. You're a one-woman SWAT team."

She was mollified by his praise, but it didn't change the situation between them. It didn't help to find Ruby, either. "Except that the SWAT team always succeeds, at least on TV."

"We're down, not out. Ruby's here somewhere," he said, gazing around the dark lane and back at the hotel.

Jennie looked around, too. "We'll find her," she said, with a determined squaring of her chin.

"And when we do, there'll be a bonus in it for you."

"This one's on the house," she said, and turned to leave. She was offended that he'd mention money at a time like this.

His hand on her arm detained her. "That was gauche of me. I'm sorry."

"I'll blame it on Hollywood. I'm sure money can buy anything there."

Wes shook his head, gazing at her. Moonlight reflected in his eyes, and painted shadows on his face. "Not everything. Not even in Hollywood." One hand reached out and took hers. Jennie instinctively withdrew.

"Don't worry. I'm not going to attack. Come on, we'll go in."

They heard an angry hissing, and turned to see that the cat had returned. It was crouched, with its fur standing on end.

"If that's a rat, I'm getting out of here!" Jennie exclaimed, and instinctively moved closer to Wes. His arm went around her shoulder protectively. He stood, rigid, staring ahead. The cat made a lunge, and suddenly they heard a frightened animal yelp.

Wes was the first to recognize the chihuahua's voice. "Ruby!" he exclaimed, and ran forward to rescue her with Jennie hard at his heels.

He scooped the shivering little bundle into his arms, as the cat darted off. Ruby made frightened sounds as she snuggled into the warmth of his arms. "She's freezing. We'd better get her inside."

When they turned to leave, Ruby straightened up, yelping in dismay. From between the cans, another little dog slunk forward, whining. In contrast to Ruby's smooth outline, this one looked like a bundle of cut wool. It was long-haired, with patches of hair sticking out over its eyes and around its nose. It came forward, tail wagging and big dark eyes imploring.

"Oh, isn't he cute!" she exclaimed, and picked it up. It gave her glove a quick lick before turning to howl amorously at Ruby.

Wes chucked Ruby under the chin. "This is only a guess, but I'd say Ruby has found herself a boyfriend." He grinned.

"I wonder where he came from. This is a toy Yorkshire terrier. He must be someone's pet. It's a valuable dog, and in good condition. We'll take it along, too," she said, and they went into the hotel, flushed with victory and in high spirits.

Both dogs became frantic, taking in the divine aromas swirling around Pierre's kitchen. Pierre filled Ruby's silver bowl, and Ruby graciously allowed her companion to share the feast. They both looked as pleased as punch as they stood together, tails wagging merrily, as they gorged themselves.

"You'd better take Ruby up to Blanche," Jennie said.

"I'll call her right away," he said, picking up Pierre's phone.

R.K. answered and was relieved to hear the news that Ruby was found. "Good work. It'll be a surprise for Blanche in the morning. I've finally convinced her to take her sleeping pill, Wes. She's just conked out. I'm leaving now. I think it's better not to disturb her."

"Then the media have left?"

"Ten minutes ago. I plan to catch the eleven o'clock news. I suggest you do likewise. Blanche was terrific."

"Come down to Jennie's office before you turn in, R.K. We have some planning to do. I need your imagination."

"I'll be right there."

When the dogs had eaten, Wes carried Ruby and Jennie took the toy terrier up to her office. She notified Mr. Simon immediately. He came racing in, followed by R.K. Benson.

"What's that?" R.K. asked, staring at the terrier.

"Just what you think," Wes laughed. "We caught them together, not quite *in flagrante delicto*, but wearing the faces of sin."

R.K. frowned. "Do we tell Blanche and the press?" he asked doubtfully. "I don't think Blanche will like this. She keeps Ruby on a short leash, metaphorically speaking. Who knows what this pair have been up to?"

They all looked at the dogs. Their satisfied air and mutual amorous looks told pretty clearly what they'd been up to.

Wes tilted his head to one side, thinking. "It's going to be an anticlimax if we just report Ruby wandered back to the hotel on her own. You know the rule for a good melodrama. A strong ending sends them away satisfied. Don't raise any expectations you can't fulfill.''

"We could go with a dognapping," R.K. said. "Ruby escaped, to come racing back to Blanche. It'll get us more ink. Page one. You can't buy that sort of coverage.''

"Not at my hotel you don't!" Mr. Simon objected. "How will it make our security look? People will be afraid to bring their children.''

"You're right," Wes agreed.

"Tell the truth. What's the big deal?" Mr. Simon asked. "We're talking about a dog here, not a virgin daughter.''

"I know it sounds absurd," Wes explained, "but Ruby is like a daughter to Blanche.''

"Even daughters are attracted to the opposite sex," Simon said reasonably.

Jennie examined the toy terrier and said, "I'd say Ruby did pretty well for herself. This is no commoner, he's a nice little pooch. I wonder who he belongs to. I think I'll call the pound.''

"Do please get rid of it," Simon said. "And meanwhile, let's call someone to take them both for a bath. The stench!''

Jennie took the dogs out and gave the instructions to one of the porters. Then she went back to her office to call the pound, Unfortunately, it wasn't open at that hour of the night. The others were still talking, so she called the police to ask if they'd had any reports of missing pets.

"Are you kidding, lady?" the policeman answered irritably. "We've had ten calls since six o'clock, when the pound closes. Everything from a German shepherd to Blanche Laure's chihuahua. Also the mayor's toy Yorkshire. A pedigreed mutt yet. It has more blue ribbons than

Mark Spitz. Hizzonner—that's the dog's name—jumped out of the car while the mayor was cutting some store ribbon downtown this afternoon. It's probably been run over by now.''

''No, it hasn't. I have him here.'' She quickly reviewed the situation. She'd find out what story Wes settled on before announcing that Ruby was back, too, with a companion. ''Don't worry about Hizzonner. I'll call you back,'' she said, and hung up before he could ask who was speaking. A wicked grin lit her face.

Wes saw it and just stood a moment, gazing. This was a side of Jennie he hadn't seen before. There was a trace of the hellion in her. Getting to know her hadn't been easy. Between business arrangements and the constant bickering, there hadn't been much chance for fun. While R.K. and Simon discussed their options, he strolled over to join her. ''You look like Lady Macbeth. What plan are you hatching?''

She looked at Simon, and beckoned Wes closer with one finger. He added flirt to her list of personas. Something about the way she crooked her finger and revealed that impish smile ... He stood with his back blocking off the others to give them privacy.

''I'm improvising,'' she said, releasing a gurgling laugh. ''How does a romantic ending for the saga of Ruby's melodrama strike you?''

''I'm all in favor of romance,'' he murmured. His voice was husky with longing. ''Blanche wouldn't want Ruby's reputation sullied by a runaway match with just any old hound, though,'' he said, feeling embarrassed at the admission.

''How about a bona fide celebrity dog? Would that remove the aura of sleaze?''

"It would say something for Ruby's taste, at least. What have you found out?"

A gurgle of girlish laughter caught in her throat, and the tantalizing dazzle of green eyes left him weak. "Hizzonner—that's the Yorkshire's name—"

"The name sounds familiar—it's the mayor—his honor."

"You're too quick!" she pouted. "Don't spoil my story. Hizzonner *is* the mayor's dog. A very high-class fella. Pedigreed, wins show ribbons, everything. You've got to admit, Wes, it would be a boffo ending!" The innate absurdity of what they were discussing overcame her and Jennie collapsed with laughter.

An answering rumble started deep in Wes's chest, which continued its way upwards till he was laughing aloud.

"What's so funny?" R.K. called.

Jennie and Wes just looked at each other and started laughing again. "We're trying to make a lady of Ruby," Wes said, finally telling the story.

Mr. Simon considered it for suitability, then posed a question. "But will the mayor go for it?"

"A month before an election?" Jennie reminded him. "You bet he'll go for it. As R.K. said, 'you can't buy that kind of publicity'."

"She's right," R.K. said. "Free TV coverage, front page pictures with Blanche, capped by a nice human interest story. My God, I'm beginning to think we could sell this scenario to Disney."

"He's already done *Lady and the Tramp*," Jennie said, and laughed again. "Mind you, Hizzonner is no tramp."

"Just between ourselves, Ruby is no lady," R.K. added. "Let's get right on it. I'll rouse Blanche. No. On second thought, I won't. Not before morning."

"Do you want to call the mayor, Mr. Simon, or shall I do it?" Jennie asked.

Mr. Simon enjoyed dealing with such people as the mayor and said he'd do it.

"Try to get him to agree to picking up Hizzonner tomorrow morning. We'll need time to call in the media," R.K. said.

"I'll take him home with me tonight, if that'll help," Jennie offered, "The mayor might not be eager to leave home in this weather, as long as he knows his dog is safe."

The mayor was delighted to learn Hizzonner was safe. He was also fully alive to the potential of free publicity in the scheme. R.K., who seemed to be in charge of logistics and promotion, decided he'd wait until morning before calling the media. Jennie called the police, informing them both dogs were safe, to save them further looking.

R.K. rubbed his hands, "Well, another crisis handled. Shall we call it a night?"

"I'll just run down and warn Pierre not to tell anyone we've recovered Ruby," Jennie said. She meant to cadge something to eat, too.

"Hurry back," Wes said. "We'll have to celebrate this victory with some of the hotel's excellent champagne."

"It's on the house!" Mr. Simon said, in an uncharacteristic fit of good humor. He was so relieved to have avoided scandal that he felt giddy. The board of directors couldn't complain about scandal when such eminent worthies as the mayor were involved. The mayor was on good terms with the board, and sent a great deal of business their way.

In the kitchen, Jennie only waited long enough to warn Pierre and grab a leg of chicken. She didn't want to miss a minute of the celebration upstairs. But, after all, it was an anticlimax. Wes couldn't say anything personal with all the others around. He could only send her meaningful glances, and smile a disconcerting smile that made her weak inside. As she hadn't eaten dinner, one glass of champagne was all she could take. She had to drive home.

Wes helped her on with her coat, and carried Hizzonner out to her car. "I've just had an idea," he said. The dog perked up its ears, as if he was listening.

"Another one? Don't you ever stop?"

"This one involves the premiere tomorrow night. I wonder if Blanche would like to go with the mayor. Is he married?"

"No, he's a bachelor, but wouldn't he have already arranged for an escort?" she asked. Jennie was a little annoyed that Wes's mind was still on his work.

"I don't know, but it's worth looking into. If it goes, then I won't have to squire Blanche." He looked at her inquiringly. "What I'm trying to do is arrange to go with you."

Frustration welled up in Jennie. It would have been nice to have that one last evening with Wes. She was sure R.K. wouldn't mind, either, if she got him a substitute date. But there really wasn't any point to it. And why should she play second fiddle to Blanche?

"I already have a date, Wes," she said nonchalantly.

"I'll give Simon another ticket. He can get his own date."

"R.K. already arranged that. I'm going with him— R.K."

Wes blinked in surprise. When had this happened? "Oh."

"Just friends," she added.

"If that's all it is, we could get R.K. a different date." He looked to see if she was interested. To judge by the upward tilt of her chin, she looked not only uninterested but downright opposed.

"I don't like breaking dates without offering a good reason. It's kind of thoughtless, don't you think?" She looked at him, almost angrily.

"Without a good reason—yes," he said uncertainly.

"Well, there's really no reason for the switch, is there? I'm sure you can get someone else to replace Blanche if you want her to go with the mayor. I really have to go now." She unlocked the car and put Hizzonner in the back seat, where he immediately began whining piteously. "I'm bushed. It's been a long day."

Wes held the car door while she got in and fastened her safety belt. "You've been great, Jennie. Thanks for your help."

"All in a day's work," she smiled brightly, although it took a lot of effort. "Or do I mean a night's work?"

Wes just touched the palm of his hand against her cheek before she closed the door. He wanted to at least touch her. His fingers brushed the soft warmth of her cheek. "Drive carefully. I'll see you tomorrow."

"*Au revoir.*" With the last of her willpower, Jennie closed the door and drove away.

She was looking over her shoulder, shushing Hizzonner when she backed out. She didn't look at Wes. He was just standing in the cold garage, his shoulders slumped. Even when she waved goodbye, she couldn't see his face. The shadows concealed the pensive, sad expression he wore. Then he turned and wandered back to the hotel. He should be feeling jubilant. Another minor crisis had not only been overcome but turned into a coup, of sorts. Somehow it didn't feel like victory.

With Hizzonner barking up a storm in the back seat, Jennie couldn't think of anything but her driving till she

was safely home. She was cold and hungry, and too tired
to cook. She just made a big mug of hot cocoa and some
toast and sat on the sofa with Hizzonner snuggled under
her arm. She tore off bits of crust and let him eat them.

It had been an interesting day. The kind of day that
made her job worthwhile. She had done interesting things,
with interesting people. She had handled it—she'd im-
provised. She should be feeling great, instead of sitting
with a large rock on her chest.

Tomorrow was shaping up to be another killer day. The
premiere to attend to, and the mayor's visit to pick up his
Yorkshire. There'd be press there to cover that. The premiere tomorrow night. That promised to be a gala, an all-
out glamorous affair. She'd told R.K. Benson she'd meet
him at the hotel, which meant getting her outfit together
and into a garment bag tonight.

She couldn't do it. She was too tired. She'd do that tomorrow morning. For tonight, she just sat thinking, taking what comfort she could from the little furry body
beside her, its nose resting comfortably on its paws now,
its eyelids drooping. Some dream of home, or food—or
Ruby—sent a shiver of pleasure through it.

Dogs were lucky. Hizzonner would forget about his affair. Jennie knew it would take a long time to get over her
non-affair. Maybe she should have... But that wasn't the
answer, of course. Not an affair, and going to work for
Wes wouldn't be right, either, with Blanche treating her
like a serf. That burning sensation was back, in the pit of
her stomach. She could give it a name now. Jealousy. And
she wasn't even sure there was anything except business
between Wes and Blanche.

Just knowing he spent so much time around beautiful
women made her angry. No, there was no way she could
possibly subject herself to that, day in and day out.

"Time for bed, Hizzonner. Don't you have a nick-name? I'll call you Hizzie for short."

The dog looked up and snuffled. "You want to sleep on the couch? That's fine with me. See you tomorrow."

Chapter Eleven

E_{ek!"}

Jennie gave a squeal of surprise when she awoke in the morning. First she felt the moist, warm tongue on her cheek. Still groggy, she opened her eyes and saw those tufts of tawny hair and a pair of bright black eyes. The creature made a lunge at her, and she yanked the cover over her head in confusion. For one paralyzing moment, she felt she had gone mad. Then Hizzonner whined, and last night came rushing back over her like the tide.

She peeped out from under the duvet and said, "*Bonjour*, Hizzie. *Parlez-vous français?*"

The dog yapped playfully. "Sounds like dog Latin to me," she said, reluctantly throwing back the warm cover. Hizzonner sat on his haunches, waiting for attention.

"I'm taking a shower, and I don't want an audience. I don't want any chewed slippers or puddles on the floor when I come out either, *comprenez-vous?*" Hizzonner whined. "Oh, all right, I'll get you a bone or something."

Jennie didn't have any bones in the fridge, so she sacrificed a well-worn moccasin and gave it to Hizzonner to chew while she showered and dressed. The dog was trotting at her heels for every step while she got her evening gown into the garment bag and selected accessories. It was really amazing how quickly he could move on those stubby little legs.

"You look like a tumbleweed," she scolded familiarly.

Hizzonner's excitement mounted as she put on her boots and coat. Hizzie wound himself into a frenzy when he sensed that she was leaving. "Don't worry, you're coming with me. You're going to see your lady friend," she said, as she scooped the dog into her arms to go to the car.

There was a buzzing crackle of tension in the hotel when Jennie entered the marble lobby. You could sense it in the air. It was like this when something important was brewing. The employees were more alert, excited. Only presidents, royalty and movie stars caused this particular atmosphere. Ridiculous to put movie stars in that category, but they really generated just as much public interest.

Mr. Simon had arrived before her. "The mayor is coming at ten-thirty. I'll take the dog," he said. He would also take any credit that was going. "There's some mix-up with the firm that was supplying the desserts for the party tonight, Ms. Longman. Get on the blower, will you? Pierre told us he didn't need outside help, but go ahead and hire an extra pastry chef for tonight. And Ms. Laure wants to see you. Nothing urgent. You can wait till the mayor and the media have left. We're using the small reception room for the photo opportunity. See that the chairs and tables are out of the way, will you?''

"Will do. Are we serving any refreshments?''

"Only coffee and something sweet at that hour of the morning. You can see what Pierre has in the way of spare cakes or desserts.''

Jennie rushed to her office, removing her coat as she went. Hizzonner leapt from Mr. Simon's arms to follow her. She picked him up and took him back. It was going to be one of those days. What could Blanche Laure want with her? A fresh red rosebud was waiting on her desk, as it was every morning. She took a minute to arrange it on her lapel. Its fresh brightness always made her feel good. Then she picked up the phone and began work.

Jennie didn't stop for hours. Through her open door, she could see the newsmen arriving, the TV crews with cameras and lights, and the photographers and reporters with their pads and pens. It was much later, closer to eleven than ten-thirty when Blanche and the mayor arrived. R.K. Benson had phoned and asked her to alert him when the mayor's limo arrived. He didn't want Blanche to be the one waiting.

"So just give me a dingle in Blanche's room, okay? She always insists on her grand entrance, you know," R.K. said. "Did you catch her on the news last night?''

"No, I forgot," Jennie exclaimed. She had planned to watch it.

"If everyone had your lack of interest in us, we'd go broke. You won't forget our date tonight, I hope?''

"I'm counting the hours, R.K.''

"Me, too. We're only saying that because it's true," he laughed, then hung up.

Jennie called the switchboard, asking to be notified when the mayor arrived. At ten forty-five, she got her call and duly informed R.K. Wes answered. She felt a little spurt of annoyance that he was with Blanche, too. "The mayor's here," she said briskly.

"Good. She'll be right down."

That's all. They both hung up without saying goodbye. It was that kind of a day, too. No frills, no time for chitchat, just business. Jennie was on the phone cajoling and threatening the supplier of six dozen petits fours, chocolate-dipped strawberries and a charlotte russe when Blanche swept into the lobby. Through her open door, Jennie noticed that the star was wearing emerald green, and carrying Ruby in one arm. Blanche looked magnificent. She had probably spent hours with her makeup and her hairdresser.

Whatever the proceedings were in the small reception room, Jennie wouldn't see unless she remembered to watch the news that night. R.K. stopped in to report.

"Blanche was great, as usual. There hasn't been her kind of charisma since Marilyn. She was a bit before my time, of course. I thought the mayor went a little overboard to say the incident cemented international relations between the States and Canada. But then he's a campaigning politician. They're as phony as some Hollywood stars."

"Yeah, there's a lot of it going around," Jennie agreed.

She poured herself a cup of coffee and offered R.K. one. "I'm due for a break," she said. "So, how did the lovers behave?"

"How did you know?" he demanded. "They hit it off like crackers and cheese. Or do I mean thunder and lightening. Blanche provided the lightening, it goes without saying."

Jennie blinked in confusion. "What?"

"The lovers—Blanche and your mayor."

"I meant the dogs."

"Oh, fine. It was a battle to keep them apart. I was wondering how you knew Wes had arranged a date between the dog lovers for the premiere . . . Blanche will be decorating His Honor's arm."

Jennie looked interested. "The mayor is going along with it?"

"Go along with it? He grabbed at it. What politician wouldn't? They do sincerely seem to like each other, though."

"Who will Wes be taking to the premiere?" she asked casually.

"He didn't say. It won't be any problem for him," R.K. said. "Oh, and about our date—I'll meet you here around seven?"

"That'll be fine. I brought my drop-dead gown." She nodded toward the garment bag.

Jennie's phone rang, and when she hung up she said, "I have to make an urgent call, R.K. I won't be a minute." As soon as she finished her call, the phone rang again.

"This is as bad as Hollywood. I'll let you get on with your telephone Ping-Pong. See you tonight," R.K. said, and left.

About ten minutes and five phone calls later there was a tap at her door and Jennie glanced up. The door was already ajar. It opened and Blanche Laure peeped her head in. Then she stepped in, still holding Ruby. At close range, her famous face actually looked quite old. Her eyes looked tired beneath the false lashes. The suspiciously firm chin hinted at plastic surgery. It didn't match the creases in her cheeks. But somehow none of it mattered. She was Blanche Laure, she was stupendous, and the only possible reaction was one of awe.

"Ms. Laure!" Jennie said, suddenly finding herself on her feet without knowing she had arisen.

"Just come to give you my thanks. Wes told me you found Ruby last night." Ruby yelped a welcome. "Such a lot of bother I've caused you. I really am desperately sorry, dear." She opened a large purse, pulling out an envelope. "I want you to have this." She offered Jennie the envelope.

Jennie thought it contained money, a reward. "That isn't necessary, Ms. Laure," she said.

"I insist. It's a keepsake. Thank you again, dear."

Blanche, a vision of loveliness, turned and swept gracefully from the office. She didn't knock anything over this time. Jennie opened the envelope, then pulled out the contents. It was a small photograph of Blanche, autographed, no doubt, by R.K. Jennie shook her head and tossed it in a drawer. "That really wasn't necessary, Ms. Laure," she said, closing the drawer.

Jennie had not spoken to Wes all day. It was a particularly grueling day for him, as well, of course. He spent some time at the theater where the film was to be previewed that evening. The police were there, to discuss traffic and safety arrangements with him. He spoke to the theater manager, the projectionist and other employees, to ensure there'd be no hitches that evening.

As he returned to the hotel in a taxi, Wes realized that those ten minutes were the longest he'd been sitting down since he got up that morning. And that included lunch. But everything was going just fine. No trouble that he could see. Blanche was in a grateful mood after the recovery of Ruby. Best of all, he'd gotten the mayor to squire her, which left him free that evening.

R.K. wouldn't object if he stole his date. In fact, if he knew how the situation stood, he'd suggest it himself. Wes

suspected, however, that Jennie would object very much
to any such high-handed tactic. And he didn't want Jennie in one of her pugnacious, objecting moods. He wanted
her full of fun and laughter, as she'd been the night before when she had whitewashed Ruby's reputation. He
wanted her eyes shining with laughter... and love.

Maybe the leading lady treatment, roses and champagne, was the first step? Except that R.K. said she wasn't
going home before the premiere, and receiving four dozen
roses in her office just might embarrass or annoy her.
When Jennie was annoyed, she was impossible. Keep it
light. She thought he was arrogant and overbearing. Show
her he was just as vulnerable and modest as she was. But
how? He could go, hat in hand, and ask modestly if she
had a friend who might go to the premiere with him. He'd
seem like an ordinary fellow, a little helpless, a stranger in
town besides. She'd take pity, then she would invite him
to accompany her and R.K.

Maybe he could send her one dozen roses. No, not
Blanche's flower, something different. Something as sweet
and natural as she was. Hyacinths, those fragrant, delicate harbingers of spring, were his own favorite. He
stopped at the flower shop in the hotel and examined the
wares for a long time. The hyacinths only came in pots,
not cut. He chose a large pot, with waxy white, pink and
violet hyacinths growing in a pleasing jumble. They would
perfume her office and remind her of him.

"Do you want a card sent with the plant?" the clerk
asked.

"No, I'll deliver it myself. Put it on my bill—Adler
from Olympia."

The clerk smiled. As if she didn't know! "Yes, Mr
Adler." She began placing it in the long paper protector.

"I'll take it just as it is," he said.

A moment later he was tapping at Jennie's office door. It was five o'clock, and at the dog end of a long, busy day, Jennie felt like a dishrag. She wanted nothing but to sink into a warm tub and relax for half an hour. She was too tired to rise to greet whoever had come to harass her. "Come in," she called.

The door opened, and Wes entered, carrying the flowers. Jennie wasn't happy that he was seeing her all frazzled, with her lipstick worn away and her face probably gray from fatigue. Not that Wes looked much better himself. He looked as if he'd been up for a month.

"I've brought you a thank-you bouquet," he said, and set it on her desk. "I hope you like hyacinths. They're my favorite."

The sweet perfume was strong at this close range. "Thank you. They're lovely. They always remind me of spring. My mom has them in her garden." She was pleasantly surprised at Wes's taste. Simple, yet elegant. After a moment's thought, she realized she shouldn't be surprised. Wes wasn't like some of the other Hollywood celebrities. He didn't use a showy wardrobe, or ridiculous jargon.

"Can I sit a minute, or are you busy?" he asked.

"I've been romancing the phone all day. I'm enjoying the calm before the storm. Everything's ready for tonight. I don't have to do anything for the next hour except get myself ready for the party. Take a load off your feet. You look bushed." She smiled.

"I am. It's been one of those days."

"Tell me about it," she said, sighing. "Are you all set for tonight?"

"I have a clean tux in my room, a fresh razor to make my face presentable. I meant to get a haircut, but somehow there wasn't time." He ran a hand nervously over his beautiful black hair.

Jennie felt her palm tingle vicariously. It would be soft, smooth. "I had some hope of getting to the hairdresser myself, but I guess I'll have to go with the braid."

"No!" His protest came out in a loud, imperative voice. "It—it looks better loose. I mean—I suits you. Not that the braid isn't attractive, too," he added in confusion.

Jennie began tidying her desk. "That must be the director coming out in you. If you hurry, you can still get to the barber. He doesn't close till six."

"Actually, I have a more pressing problem," he said, trying to look helpless.

"Suit need cleaning?" she joked. There was no answering smile. Jennie's heart plunged. "What has she done now?"

"She? Oh, you mean Blanche. No, no, this has nothing to do with Blanche."

Jennie allowed herself one snippy comment. "That's a change."

"She's not so bad really. No, my problem is, I don't have a date for the prom—er, premiere." A disastrous slip! Was he overdoing the helpless young man bit? He looked at Jennie for her reaction.

Her green eyes narrowed. He'd do anything to get what he wanted. She'd been warned of that before. He still wanted her. "Careless of you," she said unconcernedly. "You've known since this morning that Blanche is going with the mayor. Why didn't you make some arrangement?"

"I've been so busy, and I don't know anyone in town. I was wondering if—" Her stiff jaw dared him to say it. "If you have a friend, someone who might be willing to go with me at the last minute." Well, he had surprised her at least, caught her off guard. It was too late for her to get him a blind date. She'd have to invite him to join her and R.K.

"I bet Blanche wouldn't mind two escorts," she suggested.

At least the idea of a threesome had gotten through to her. "The mayor would though. Since he's obliging us by escorting Blanche, it would be dirty pool for me to clutter up their act. Any other ideas?" he asked hopefully.

Jennie shook her head, half suspecting she was being cornered. "Yes, I have an idea. It goes against my principles to do it. You've got to promise to behave yourself, Wes," she said sternly.

He looked offended. "I'm not a savage, you know. Have I behaved heinously till now?"

"No, not heinously—till now." The gleam of amusement was back in her eyes.

"I'll be a model of decorum. What time are we meeting?"

"I'm meeting R.K. here at seven. Why don't you join us here?"

"I'll be on time," he promised rashly.

"Me, too, if you'll leave me now and let me make my last few phone calls."

Wes rose, studying her with softly gazing eyes. "I look forward to tonight."

"Thanks again for the flowers."

"They reminded me of you," he said. Then he left.

Jennie examined the hyacinths in confusion. They certainly weren't four dozen roses. As far as she was concerned, they were better. Hyacinths seemed more sincere, more romantic. Then she lifted the phone to call Beckie

Hamilton. Beckie was ecstatic to hear she had a date with
Wes Adler.

"How come he didn't invite you?" Beckie asked.

"I already had a date. We're all meeting at seven at the
hotel. And it's very fancy," she said in a haughty tone.
"It'll be a chance to wear your glitzy gold gown. See
you."

Jennie finally left her office and went up to the vacant
room she was using to change. That was one of the perks
of her job, a free room downtown when she needed it. She
had her soak in a perfumed tub, which felt refreshing.

It was fun, getting all dressed up. The flame red of her
gown contrasted dramatically with her white shoulders. It
was strapless, clinging to her breasts and nipping in
sharply to define her small waist. The orchid R.K. sent her
was white with just a blush of color at the center, so it
didn't clash. When she unbraided her hair, she saw the
moisture had set it into an interesting cascade of waves,
with loose tendrils curling in front.

She brushed it out but didn't rebraid it. Wes had seemed
very decided on that point. Didn't he like the way she wore
her hair? A little frown puckered her brow. What did she
care what he thought? She was just wearing it loose because it happened to look nice tonight, kind of festive.
That's all.

She took her time over her makeup, carefully applying
silver eye shadow to lend her eyes a touch of evening
drama. Her only jewelry was a pair of dangling grape-
cluster rhinestones at her ears. When she was all finished, she had a whole ten minutes to herself. She took a
can of soda pop from the little fridge and sat down with
her feet up to relax. Her arches ached from running all
day, but a tingling excitement overcame her fatigue. Af-

ter ten minutes passed, she picked up her evening bag and
went to the elevator.

It was seven on the dot, and Wes was already there at
the door, waiting. R.K. hadn't arrived yet, neither had
Beckie. Jennie examined Wes as she advanced. He looked
handsome, so debonair that she felt like throwing herself
into his arms. The dark, formal suit was a perfect com-
plement to his elegantly tall figure. He hadn't gotten to the
barber, after all. His sideburns were still longish, and at
the back his hair met his collar. What a nicely shaped head
he had.

His head turned, and he came forward to meet her. She
was a little surprised he hadn't brought Beckie a corsage.
But it was a last minute date, and she knew Beckie
wouldn't mind.

"R.K. should be here in a minute," Wes said. But the
eyes examining her sent a different message. They caressed her pale face, lingering on the halo of gleaming
chestnut hair, before making a quick trip over her chic
gown. Her white shoulders were dainty, with creamy,
perfect skin. "I'm glad you wore your hair like that," he
said, flickering his gaze again to her face.

Jennie felt he was stroking her with his eyes. Something inside her turned soft, like butter in the sun.

"Shall we wait in your office?" Wes asked. His voice
matched his eyes, it was blurred with some intense emotion.

She said, "Sure," in a breathless voice.

R.K. arrived immediately. The only extravagance he
allowed himself was a ruffled shirt front. Now that he was
an assistant to the director, he meant to dress the part. He
looked fine, and the look he gave Jennie told her he approved of her, too.

"You took me at my word, J.M. When you dress up, you really put on all the bells and whistles. The mayor just went up to Blanche's room. Shall we go to the cocktail party and wait for them?"

"We can't go yet!" Jennie said.

"Blanche won't be down for another half hour," Wes said. "Why don't we have some wine in here first, just the three of us. A private party." And soon just the two of us, he thought.

Jennie said, "I think Beckie would prefer to go right on to the big do as soon as she arrives."

"Beckie?" Wes shot her a look of confusion. "What the devil—"

Jennie hadn't told him who she was getting for his blind date, but she thought he would have guessed. "Beckie Hamilton. You remember, we met her at the art show."

"I thought we mentioned a threesome," he said accusingly.

As they spoke, Jennie looked to the door spying Beckie's approach. "Here she is now." She went to the door to greet her.

Wes took care of introductions, which left Jennie time to think. Threesome? He'd asked her to get him a date. What was going on here? At least he was behaving politely, being very friendly to Beckie.

"Can we go to the party now?" Beckie asked. "I'm just *dying* to see Blanche Laure. And I hear her costar David Store is here, too. Those eyes!" she sighed.

"He wears colored contacts," R.K. said. "His eyes are really a washed-out blue. He looks like something from outer space on film."

"Killjoy," Beckie grouched.

They went in a group to the cocktail party. Wes continued to behave properly. He introduced Beckie and Jennie to all the visiting stars, which was much more interesting for them than meeting the producers and technical support staff.

"I think I've died and gone to heaven," Beckie said. "David Store touched my hand. I may never wash it again. His eyes are beautiful."

"He was wearing the contacts," R.K. decided.

Beckie sighed. "Lucky contacts."

"You sound like a teenage groupie," Jennie laughed.

"I do, don't I?" she agreed. "This is my first brush with film celebrities. And probably my last. I mean to wallow in it."

They all nibbled on the hors d'oeuvre and called it dinner. No one, including Beckie, had bothered to eat. It was not much later before a hush fell over the crowd as they turned their attention on Blanche making her grand entrance on the mayor's arm. She wore a long, white glistening gown, carefully designed to conceal the aging surface of her neck and bony composition of her shoulders. She accessorized her formal with a diamond brooch and earrings. The new sapphire ring was in evidence, too, a large, glittering stone.

There was general noise and confusion until the party piled into a stream of limousines for the trip to the theater. It was just like the Academy Awards. Fans thronged the streets to stare at the stars. Amidst the noise and lights and general pandemonium, Beckie just smiled mutely at Jennie. It was obviously a dream come true for her. Jennie's pleasure was diluted by the fact that it was Beckie hanging on Wes's arm, not herself.

She had been thinking about his peculiar reaction at the hotel, and realized he thought he was going to the premiere with her and R.K. They could have found a few private moments if she hadn't invited Beckie. Why didn't he tell her that was what he meant? She couldn't really complain. He had asked her last night to go with him.

When they were all seated in the theater, the house became silent. Music swelled and the shimmering gold curtains, lit by multicolored lights from below, opened. "An Olympia presentation. Blanche Laure, starring in *Orphan of the Storm*." Blanche, of course, had star billing. "Produced by Wescott Adler, directed by Wescott Adler." Jennie felt a burst of pride. Wes sat beside her in the darkened theater, with Beckie on his other side.

He was tense with anxiety. This was his opening night, and she sensed that his nerves were drawn wire-tight. Wescott Adler, nervous! She leaned toward him whispering, "Relax. It's going to be terrific."

His hand seized hers and squeezed. In the darkness, she saw his nervous smile. "It better be. I've got thirty million bucks tied up in it. Wish me luck."

Thirty million dollars! How could he live under such strain? No wonder he was a little brusque and arrogant at times. Wes must have been on thorns all week, worrying about these two hours that he was facing now. Blanche was sitting in the row in front of them, a few seats away so that Jennie had a three-quarter view of her face. She was strained with anxiety, too. It was a tough life, being an actress. You had to smile in public on an occasion like this. Her lips were compressed in a thin line, that emphasized the creases in her cheeks. It must be awful to be growing old and losing your beauty, especially when your face was your major asset. She felt a stab of pity for Blanche.

The tension began seeping into Jennie. Her throat went dry, and she wondered what they'd all do if the movie was a flop. She looked at Wes. He smiled wanly. "Are you going to be all right?" she asked.

"Maybe, if I have something to hold on to."

They arranged their arms so that neither R.K. nor Beckie realized they were holding hands. The movie began, and from the first moments there was little doubt that it was going to be a winner. Whatever magic tricks the makeup man had performed on Blanche, he had made her look fabulous. And probably the cameraman had used one of those lens filters to soften the harsh edges. It wouldn't work much longer. Blanche was wise to take *Mother Courage*, to start portraying older women.

After an hour, Wes didn't really need anyone to hold on to, but he still held Jennie's hand. He had seen the film a dozen times and knew every scene, every shot by heart. He knew he liked it, and since everyone else did, too, he allowed his eyes to drift from the screen. Blanche was replaying her role, even mouthing some of the lines. She was a real fire horse. It was time she took the bit between her teeth and tackled a role that really tested her mettle.

He glanced at Jennie. How young and sweet she looked, like a little girl at the circus with her eyes glued on the action. But underneath her youthful innocence, she was made of surprisingly sterner stuff. He liked that, too. His fingers tightened unconsciously. She didn't notice, but she squeezed back without thinking.

A roar of applause went up when the movie finished. Blanche rose and took a bow, then gestured dramatically at Wes. He stood and Blanche blew him a kiss. Jennie saw the tears in Blanche's eyes. Was she acting or were they real? No one knew, not even Blanche. Compliments filled the air as the crowd streamed out to the waiting limousines to return to the hotel. When the party began, Jennie thought she had never seen so much kissing and so many people calling each other darling in loud, insincere voices.

"Darling, you were marvelous!" R.K. said, giving Blanche a big bear hug.

"Too kind, darling. It was rather good, wasn't it? Wes, darling! We've done it again. I can hardly wait to start our next." It was Wes's turn to hug and kiss her.

Her costar, David Store, called her darling. Blanche called the mayor darling. At one point, Jennie even saw her hug Mr. Simon, and say, "This darling man has taken such good care of me and Ruby. I would have perished without him. Would you be a dear and bring my Ruby down? She adores parties. She's locked in my bathroom. I promised her she could have a tiny glass of champagne."

Mr. Simon passed the request, or royal command, on to Jennie. "Would you mind, Ms. Longman? Ms. Laure requested it. She's marvelous, isn't she?" he asked, with a besotted smile on his face. "I'd like to get an autographed picture for my office. She has some with her, I believe."

"I think I can arrange that, Mr. Simon," Jennie replied. Easy as opening her desk drawer.

"You might as well call me P.S.," he said. He was back in the camp.

Jennie was happy to get away from the noise and confusion of the party for a few moments. She found Ruby asleep on Blanche's bed. She was wearing a rhinestone collar, and nail polish on her nails for the party. Poor thing. That was no way to treat a dog. When she brought the dog down, Blanche clutched it, kissing its moist, little nose. She forgot to thank Jennie. "We did it. Congratulate me, Ruby," she cooed.

The dog licked her chin, which made Blanche laugh. Jennie found it strange that it was only her dog that

Blanche called by name. It meant more to her than all those adoring fans.

She mentioned it to R.K. a little later. "It's lonesome at the top," he said philosophically. "Everyone admires Blanche. She's a national treasure, but she's not an easy person to get close to. Blanche is more than a woman. She's an institution, like the flag, or a monarchy. Or income taxes," he added, thinking of her less lovable qualities.

"I guess it'd be pretty hard for her not have a good opinion of herself when everyone makes such a fuss over her."

"She's always playing the star, even when the cameras stop. Of course, it's the only life she knows. She's been a star since she was a child, grew up in the business. In this game, you have to play the role. Make ridiculous demands. If one actress gets a five-seater limo, the next one wants a stretch limo. If one gets a mil a picture, the next one holds out for a mil and a half. It's the pecking order thing. You have to hang tough. And speaking of hanging tough, how are you making out in your negotiations with Wes?"

"I told you, no deal."

"Is that why you pulled that little stunt on him tonight—inviting Beckie along? That one really floored him. He thought he was coming with us. Yours truly," he gave a little bow, "was all set to discreetly disappear when it was time for him to take you home."

Jennie felt a stab of disappointment. "It wasn't a stunt. It was a misunderstanding. Wes asked me to get him a date," she scowled.

"It's still not too late," he said. "I can entertain Beckie for half an hour, if you and Wes want to—"

"No, that's not necessary, thanks," she said brusquely.

R.K. seemed genuinely bewildered. "What have you got against the guy? He's crazy about you, J.M."

She looked at him doubtfully. "I'm crazy about him, too, if you want the truth. But I couldn't live like this. This is like a Roman orgy."

"This only happens once a year. You wouldn't judge New Orleans by Mardi Gras, would you?"

She pondered it a moment. "No, that wouldn't be fair."

"Think about it. And now I'm going to give Blanche's arm a rest and take Ruby upstairs. Can you get along without me for a few minutes?"

"I'll manage."

They stood near the doorway. Jennie looked at the noisy scene and knew she had had enough. She'd go to her office, then catch R.K. on his way back down to tell him she was going home.

Across the room, Wes watched her steal away and went after her. He didn't know what he could say or do to convince her, but he knew this was his last chance.

Jennie slumped in her chair and drew out the picture of Blanche, to have R.K. add "to Paul," before she left. She'd give it to Mr. Simon after the Olympia party left. She gazed at the photograph. Blanche Laure, a legend. She decided to keep it, after all. Blanche wasn't so bad. She was the product of her environment, like everyone else.

It wasn't Blanche she had to compete with. It was a whole life-style. But as R.K. said, it wasn't always like this. Mardi Gras only lasted a few days. What was the rest of Wes's life really like? She'd probably never know. The scent of hyacinths perfumed the air, reminding her of him. These simple flowers were his favorite, too.

She had judged Wes by the few days she'd known him, but there was obviously more to his life than glamour and movie stars. There was all the tremendous pressure of raising and risking the money, and the technical end of moviemaking that she knew absolutely nothing about. Apart from that, even a dedicated movie director had a private life, too. She found herself wondering what he did in his idle hours.

When Wes appeared silently at her door, Jennie sat gazing into the distance with a pensive smile on her face. "Penny for your thoughts," he said, walking in.

Jennie gave a little jump of surprise. "Oh, you frightened me, Wes."

"Sorry. I noticed you slip out, and was afraid you were leaving the party. I wanted to say goodbye and thanks, before you left."

"But you'll still be here tomorrow morning!" she exclaimed in panic. A devastating sense of loss engulfed her to consider a future without Wes. To come into the hotel and find it quiet, with no emergency to handle for the Olympia group. Oh, there'd be the other normal business, of course, but it seemed hollow in comparison to the events of the past few days.

"We don't leave till noon," he replied. His dark eyes studied her. "You almost sound as if you care, as if you'll miss us," he added on a questioning note.

Jennie just looked, with a telling glance. He went to her desk, and saw she was holding Blanche's photograph. "I see Blanche has given you a keepsake," he added, amused.

"I was thinking of giving it to Mr. Simon, but I was so impressed with her tonight, I think I'll keep it as a memento of this visit."

Wes's hand reached for the picture. He glanced at it, then set it aside, to take Jennie's fingers in his. His voice, when he spoke, was husky. "I had a different keepsake in mind. This.'' He drew her up from her chair and pulled her into his arms.

There were a dozen, a hundred things he had meant to say to convince her first. He meant to give her the diamond ring he had stashed in his pocket. He wanted to explain things to her. But when he felt her light, shallow breaths on his cheek, saw the gleam of love in her eyes, her lips trembling with anticipation, he knew the moment had come. Details could be settled later. Instinct told him to forge ahead while the moment was right.

His arms tightened inexorably around her, then their lips touched. He knew in his soul this was as right as anything could be. His lips firmed, and he began to kiss her ruthlessly, all gentleness forgotten in the moment's passion.

Jennie felt the world spin around her in a heady, dizzying whirl. The unexpected embrace seemed as unreal as the rest of this spectacular evening. It seemed bigger than life, too big for her to handle. She felt she was drowning in it. Wes's lips were relentlessly taunting hers. She realized her arms had wrapped themselves tightly around his neck, as she wanted so desperately to draw him closer.

A moist flicker at her lips warned her the kiss was passionately escalating. Closing her lips, she gave way to the persuasion of his tongue. He took full possession of her mouth in an assault of sinuous strokes that left her weak with longing. This was exactly what she had been trying to avoid. She pushed him away, gasping.

''Too bad I can't put that little keepsake in a frame.'' Her voice trembled with agitation.

Dark eyes caressed her. His face was soft with desire. ''You can't confine love to narrow boundaries, Jen,'' he said huskily. She heard the word love, and something inside her turned to water. She looked away, in an attempt to hide her feelings.

Wes lifted one hand and cupped her chin, tilting her head up, forcing her to meet his gaze. His other hand settled on the naked flesh of her shoulder. It felt feverishly hot. Was it her or his hand? Or had the contact conducted that much heat?

"Love's a great, unwieldy thing, isn't it?" he asked softly, while his fingers massaged her shoulder with sure, firm strokes. "It comes lumbering onstage at the worst moment, like a runaway bear, and upsets all our plans. The best thing is to deal with it, so that we can get on with our lives."

"You know how I feel about sharing your life, Wes," she reminded him, but uncertainly. Her flickering lashes were an invitation to persuade her otherwise.

"I wouldn't even ask you to work for me. That was never what I wanted, Jen. It was just an excuse, a pretext for us to be together, to get to know each other a little better before I asked you to marry me. I was sure I loved you, but I knew you needed time."

Her heart raced with joy. "Really?" she asked uncertainly.

A gentle smile tugged at his lips. "Really. I even took the precarious step of—buying this." He slid his hand in his pocket and brought out the diamond ring. It caught the fire from her lamp and reflected a prism of dancing colors. "I was forced to purchase that sapphire for Blanche because this diamond was meant for you. She found out I'd bought a ring, and assumed it was for her. Since I didn't want to offend her, I got her one, too. Not a diamond, of course, whatever you heard. Yours is prettier, don't you think? I've been trying to give it to you for a couple of days now. The moment and place never seemed right.'' He slid it on her finger, and they both looked at it a moment in uncertain silence.

She remembered their meeting in the crowded bar, and the way he had fondled her left hand. He had meant to give it to her then, when R.K. came rushing in with his disastrous announcement and Wes had turned to stone. She realized how much had hung on that premiere, that Wes's concern had not been hinging on Blanche Laure. She was sure of his love, but problems remained. She looked longingly at the beautiful ring and said, ''How can I marry you? My job's here.''

''You said you wanted to move around, work in different countries. There are fine hotels in Hollywood that could use more than one concierge.''

''But are they looking for one?''

''I—er, took the liberty of phoning a friend last night. He owns one of the most prestigious hotels in town and he has an opening.''

Jennie cast a suspicious glance at him. ''Last night I hadn't said I'd marry you.'' That mischievous smile was flirting at the edge of her lips. Wes, finding it irresistible, stole a quick kiss.

''Last night I hadn't asked you,'' he riposted. ''I like to be prepared. That's why I bought the ring. I didn't want the future of your career to stand in your way.''

''I did plan to go to California eventually,'' she said, thinking. ''Much good it will do me. Isn't your next movie in France?''

''I've learned something from you. Improvise! California has a varied terrain. I'm sure I can find a suitable location. I'd still like to do some backgrounds in Europe, but that won't take long. My main basis of operations is Hollywood. We won't be together three hundred and sixty-five days a year, but we'll keep the long distance operators busy.'' He spoke persuasively, passionately, and Jennie listened.

"We won't really be separated, just apart temporarily. My whole life's work is make-believe, and from what I've seen of yours, it's as hectic as mine. We need something solid and serene and real.''

The hand on her chin was stroking her jaw, sending shock waves along her spine. "I don't know—it's so sudden,'' she said.

"It's seemed like months to me already, the waiting,'' he said in a strained voice. "The job, whether we're together all the time—those are just details, Jen. We can work all that out between us. The question really is, do you love me?''

With her heart hammering mercilessly, Jennie looked at him, asking herself the same question. Do I love him? The answer had been staring her in the face all along. Of course, she loved him. Why else had she been on pins and needles all week? Why else had she taken such an unnatural aversion to Hollywood, and Blanche Laure? It had been a mental trick, trying to tell herself she disliked it, so she wouldn't fall in love or, worse, suffer from a broken heart. But she hadn't fooled herself.

"Well?'' he asked.

"Let's try another take on that kiss,'' she said, smiling impishly.

"Take two,'' he whispered hoarsely, kissing her again. With his lips, nibbling her neck a moment later, he murmured, "Mmm, take three.''

They were on take nine or ten when R.K. stopped in. "It looks like a wrap to me,'' he said, "Cut. You've abandoned a lady at the party, Wes. That's not like you.''

"Good lord, Beckie!'' Jennie exclaimed.

R.K. looked ready to burst with curiosity. "I'm, sure she'll forgive all when she learns the reason. There *is* a reason you're both smiling like a pair of besotted ingenues rehearsing *Romeo and Juliet*, I suppose?"

"Wrong play, R.K.," Wes said. "It's *All's Well That Ends Well*. Jennie's agreed to marry me."

He clapped his hands lightly. "Surprise, surprise. Don't think you'll escape us movie mavens entirely, J.M. The place will be crawling with impossible stars and semi-stars."

"Hey," Jennie grinned. "I handled the biggest of them all. Don't try to scare me with small potatoes after I've handled Blanche Laure."

"And Wes Adler," R.K. added roguishly.

"Let's make the announcement," Wes suggested and headed for the door, holding Jennie by the hand, drawing her after him.

"Not yet!" she protested. "I want to tell Mom first, and Mr. Simon. Besides, you don't want to spoil the premiere party with another announcement."

"This lady learns fast," R.K. said. "You'll have to up your offer, Wes. We need her at Olympia."

Wes winked at Jennie. "I'm working on that too, R.K. So far I'm batting a thousand."

"Can I just whisper it to Blanche?" R.K. asked. "She'll have to learn J.M.'s name now."

"And you'll have to learn my new initial," Jennie smiled.

"Why do you think I called you J.M., instead of J.L.? We use the first names' initials. The last ones change too often in tinsel town." Jennie and Wes shared a secret, confident smile. "Somehow, I don't think that's going to be a problem with you two," he added.

"If it looks like a problem looming on the horizon, I'll handle it," Jennie said. "That's my job."

Wes Adler whispered a mental "Amen," and the three of them rejoined the party.

* * * * *

COMING NEXT MONTH

#658 A WOMAN IN LOVE—Brittany Young
When archaeologist Melina Chase met the mysterious Aristo Drapano aboard a treasure-hunting ship in the Greek isles, she knew he was her most priceless find....

#659 WALTZ WITH THE FLOWERS—Marcine Smith
When Estella Blaine applied for a loan to build a stable on her farm, she never expected bank manager Cody Marlowe to ask for her heart as collateral!

#660 IT HAPPENED ONE MORNING—Jill Castle
A chance encounter in the park with free-spirited dog trainer Collier Woolery had Neysa Williston's orderly heart spinning. Could he convince her that their meeting was destiny?

#661 DREAM OF A LIFETIME—Arlene James
Businessman Dan Wilson needed an adventure and found one in the Montana Rockies with lovely mountain guide Laney Scott. But now he wanted her to follow his trail....

#662 THE WEDDING MARCH—Terry Essig
Feisty five-foot Lucia Callahan had had just about enough of tall, protective men, and she set out to find a husband her own size...but she couldn't resist Daniel Statler—all six feet of him!

#663 NO WAY TO TREAT A LADY—Rita Rainville
Aunt Tillie was at it again, matchmaking between her llama-ranching nephew, Dave McGraw, and reading teacher Jennifer Hale. True love would never be the same again!

AVAILABLE THIS MONTH:

"GIVE YOUR HEART TO SILHOUETTE" SWEEPSTAKES
OFFICIAL RULES

NO PURCHASE NECESSARY TO ENTER OR RECEIVE A PRIZE

To enter and join the Silhouette Reader Service, rub off the concealment device on all game tickets. This will reveal the potential value for each Sweepstakes entry number and the number of free book(s) you will receive. Accepting the free book(s) will automatically entitle you to also receive a free bonus gift. If you do not wish to take advantage of our introduction to the Silhouette Reader Service but wish to enter the Sweepstakes only, rub off the concealment device on tickets #1-3 only. To enter, return your entire sheet of tickets. Incomplete and/or inaccurate entries are not eligible for that section or section (s) of prizes. Not responsible for mutilated or unreadable entries or inadvertent printing errors. Mechanically reproduced entries are null and void.

Either way, your Sweepstakes numbers will be compared against the list of winning numbers generated at random by computer. In the event that all prizes are not claimed, random drawings will be made from all entries received from all presentations to award all unclaimed prizes. All cash prizes are payable in U.S. funds. This is in addition to any free, surprise or mystery gifts that might be offered. The following prizes are awarded in this sweepstakes:

(1)	*Grand Prize	$1,000,000	Annuity
(1)	First Prize	$35,000	
(1)	Second Prize	$10,000	
(3)	Third Prize	$5,000	
(10)	Fourth Prize	$1,000	
(25)	Fifth Prize	$500	
(5000)	Sixth Prize	$5	

*The Grand Prize is payable through a $1,000,000 annuity. Winner may elect to receive $25,000 a year for 40 years, totaling up to $1,000,000 without interest, or $350,000 in one cash payment. Winners selected will receive the prizes offered in the Sweepstakes promotion they receive.

Entrants may cancel the Reader Service privileges at any time without cost or obligation to buy (see details in center insert card).

Versions of this Sweepstakes with different graphics may be offered in other mailings or at retail outlets by Torstar Corp. and its affiliates. This promotion is being conducted under the supervision of Marden-Kane, Inc., an independent judging organization. By entering this Sweepstakes, each entrant accepts and agrees to be bound by these rules and the decisions of the judges, which shall be final and binding. Odds of winning are dependent upon the total number of entries received. Taxes, if any, are the sole responsibility of the winners. Prizes are nontransferable. All entries must be received by March 31, 1990. The drawing will take place on April 30, 1990, at the offices of Marden-Kane, Inc., Lake Success, N.Y.

This offer is open to residents of the U.S., Great Britain and Canada, 18 years or older, except employees of Torstar Corp., its affiliates, and subsidiaries, Marden-Kane, Inc. and all other agencies and persons connected with conducting this Sweepstakes. All federal, state and local laws apply. Void wherever prohibited or restricted by law.

Winners will be notified by mail and may be required to execute an affidavit of eligibility and release that must be returned within 14 days after notification. Canadian winners will be required to answer a skill-testing question. Winners consent to the use of their name, photograph and/or likeness for advertising and publicity in conjunction with this and similar promotions without additional compensation. One prize per family or household.

For a list of our most current major prizewinners, send a stamped, self-addressed envelope to: WINNERS LIST, c/o MARDEN-KANE, INC., P.O. BOX 701, SAYREVILLE, N.J. 08871

If sweepstakes entry form is missing, please print your name and address on a 3" x 5" piece of plain paper and send to:

In the U.S.	In Canada
Sweepstakes Entry	Sweepstakes Entry
901 Fuhrmann Blvd.	P.O. Box 609
P.O. Box 1867	Fort Erie, Ontario
Buffalo, NY 14269-1867	L2A 5X3

LTY-S69R

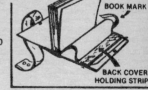